Windswept Rohm

Patrick Quin Kermott

PoorlyScribbledPages

Patrick Quin Kermott

NOTE: If you purchased this book without a cover you should be aware that this book is stolen property. It was reported as "unsold and destroyed" to the publisher, and neither the author nor the publisher has received any payment for this "stripped book."

This is a work of fiction. All of the characters, organizations, and events portrayed in this novel are either products of the author's imagination or are used fictitiously.

Windswept Rohm

Originally published in July 2012 as "Sex and Violence"

ISBN: 978-0615766140

Printed in the United States of America

First paperback edition / June 2013

http://www.poorlyscribbledpages.com

Acknowledgements

This book would not have been possible without the incredible contributions of three women, to whom I would like to deeply express my gratitude.

To Barbara Kermott: You were the first I ever told that writing was in my heart, and you were the very first to believe that I could do it.

To Kris Kermott: You taught me growing up that if we tried to shelter the world from books about sex and violence, nobody would even be allowed to read the Bible.

To Lindsay Kermott: For never giving up on your husband or this story and for never letting me give up on it either.

In loving memory of George Brandt

Prologue

Todd has been a complete and total gentleman all night long. When my friend Fabian set me up on this blind date, I was skeptical about what kind of behavior to expect. Your average guys, whether it be through their words, actions, or just by watching the eyes, make it very obvious what they're looking for. He's not like that.

Todd is both trusting and genuine. I don't carry either one of those traits and I tend to believe that the rest of the world is with me on that one. For example, he gave me his real name. I've never done that on a blind date. I always make sure that whoever sets me up on these things tells the guy that my name is Stacey of Jennifer or Bob or something along those lines. That way I can be spared the awkward moment the next day when he sends me a friend request on his favorite social networking site, whereas I generally find myself planning to just not return his calls.

So, my real name is Windswept Rohm. This date is actually the one exception to my rule. In this case, Todd knows exactly what my name is. I'm not sure he would have gone out with me otherwise.

The conversation hasn't been heavy, which is always a plus. You want to get past the small talk but when you start to hit on religion or politics then you know the night's a disaster.

We talked a bit about our families. Mine was small and tightly knit until my parents passed. His is large and just as tightly knit, maybe even more so. They still talk to each other often and get together on holidays.

Dinner was nice enough. It was a new place I'd never been to before. Uncharted territory is another risk for a blind date. It's always easier to be yourself when you're somewhere comfortable. But on the other hand, if you go to some place you enjoy and the night doesn't end well, you end up avoiding one of your favorite venues just to avoid a guy. So I didn't object when after dinner he suggested a club that was outside of my usual haunts. In this case it's not really going to make a difference.

He's amazing. Such a gentleman. We dance until the club closes and then we talk all night after that. When the night finally leads us back to my doorstep, he asks if he can call me again. I tell him he can. We exchange numbers and I kiss him on the cheek before he takes off down the walk.

I really would enjoy spending another evening with him. I don't think I've ever met anyone like him or if I ever will again. That's not the sort of thing a girl can let go of.

It'll be a real shame when I have to kill him.

Now don't be upset or anything like that. He's a great guy and I can't honestly say that I want to kill him. I really don't. I'm not some kind of psychopath that stabs a guy twenty seven times and then giggles about it all the way home. It's nothing like that at all. Despite the nice date, I'm not enjoying this in the least. It's just what needs to be done. There's a fine line between determination and addiction. I'm not addicted. I would feed you a line about being able to quit any time I wanted, but that wouldn't exactly be true. I can't quit. It's morally imperative that I don't.

But I'm getting ahead of myself. The topic

at hand is Todd. I feel bad because he doesn't know he's going to die and the chances are that he'll die having never known why. Mind you, there is a reason, and a very good one. I can't exactly stop to tell him though. If I do the whole super villain monologue thing, everything gets complicated. If he has the opportunity to cry for help, try to run, beg for mercy… it's just going to get really messy. But there is a reason. Nothing he can say will make that reason go away.

Listen to me overthinking everything, trying to justify it. I've spent too much time lost in thought. I need to go back now. Back to the doorstep where Todd left me.

I know he's standing there. I know that as soon as I came inside, he turned around and came back. I made a good enough impression. I let off enough nervous laughter and body language to make him want me and to let him think I'm okay with that. And now he stands on the doorstep, looking down, trying to gather up the courage to knock. It's only a matter of seconds now.

Four…
Three…
Two…
One…

Knock knock knock.

I know what's going to happen. I planned it down to the second. But the anticipation is still killing me.

I open the door and Todd stands there with his jaw agape. He didn't think past the knock on the door. So it's no surprise that when the words finally come they amount to nothing more than, "I... am... well... I just..."

I put my finger up to his lips and speak in that voice that I've so perfected: the sultry, sweet, seductive, innocent, confident voice that will melt his heart as it gets him hot. "Don't. I know why you came back. And maybe I shouldn't have answered the door, but in all honesty I was sitting on the floor on the other side, praying for you to knock. And when you did, I couldn't hear the voice of reason over my own heartbeat."

Yeah, it's a line. A really bad line too. But spoken in the right tone to someone looking for a line... Let's face it, the words don't matter.

His fingers brush my cheek, from the edge of my lips to the hair they end up entwined in. His palm cups the back of my head and he pulls my lips to his.

His kiss is amazing. Gentle but passionate. I wish things were different. I wish this wasn't going where it's going. But it is. It has to.

Before I know it, I'm pulling him inside. We can't keep our hands off of each other. My arms are wrapped around him, under his shirt, feeling his skin. His lips are on my neck. His fingers unbutton my blouse. Our faces practically melt into each other as I reach for the button on his pants and his hands explore what was hiding under my clothing.

And then he feels it: the prick from the point of what's tucked into the strap of my bra.

"Ah!" he says, pulling his finger in front of his face and examining the wound. He takes a deep breath through gritted teeth.

"Are you okay?" I ask, stroking his cheek and gazing longingly into his eyes.

Todd gives his finger another look and his grit teeth turn into a smile, followed by a long kiss and a tight embrace that ends with his hands caressing my back and with my leg wrapping around his.

When our lips release, he smiles again. "I'm fine," he says. "It must've been your underwire or something."

I look into his eyes again as my mouth curls into a smile of its own. I draw back a few inches, reach across my torso, and pull the short knife that was concealed in the side of my undergarments.

A look of confusion with a touch of shock flashes across his face.

I cock my head slightly to the side, my eyes grow concerned. "I hope this isn't going to be a problem," I say in the same sultry voice as before.

And with a swift jerk of my arm, a look of terror across his face, and the feel of warm, sticky liquid dripping across my fingers, I know it's not going to be a problem at all.

Windswept Rohm

Love is complicated. I can't count the times I've thought I was in love or told that I was the object of another's love. Most of those cases weren't actually love though. Lust, infatuation, appreciation, but not love. To most, love is a four letter word in the same category as countless other four letter words that are generally used to describe intercourse or the parts used to have intercourse. Real love is an emotion that has just as much to do with dedication as it does desire. Probably more, actually. My parents loved me. My mother nearly died for me on the night I was born. I think that if she had died that night, she probably would have been okay with that. God bless her. I'll never doubt that she loved me.

One

My parents left me a fair amount of money when they passed. Well, it was an obscene amount to be honest. Somehow they managed to pull off a fairy tale wedding between a model and a real estate mogul without a single flashbulb going off. They were remarkably successful in their respective careers, but they never got themselves pinched for a DUI or some kind of drunken anti-sematic rant and they were never seen coming out of ritzy clubs or sitting around with a straw up their noses.

Apparently, the best way to avoid the paparazzi is just to bore the hell out of them. You can own the world, you can appear in some way in every last magazine on the newsstand, but if you spend your free time only doing respectable things and your evenings are all at home then nobody could really care less about you.

I was a different story. At least in their eyes

I was. I had aspirations to go to an Ivy League school and be someone important like a doctor or a lawyer or a psychiatrist with a daytime television show on after Judge Judy. But as soon as I grew breasts, my parents began trying to make me into their perception of the average wealthy teenager. They were procuring fake IDs for me and sneaking me into clubs and everything else that could get me into trouble.

Dad always joked that he was trying to push me off on some eligible bachelor so that they could finally have the house to themselves. Mom insisted that they had saved all their money in case I grew up to be Lindsay Lohan or Paris Hilton and needed legal counsel every other week. Apparently, I was sorely disappointing them.

Nevertheless, they did leave me all this money, so I figure that the least I can do to honor their memories is to hit up a club every once in a while, show up at the same Starbucks every single morning and flip off the occasional photographer. It's really difficult being associated with famous, dead, boring people.

But that leads me to where I am now: Starbucks. TMZ doesn't particularly care what kind of celebrity you are or whether you might just be related to one. If they caught wind of Rick Moranis's former roommate's son-in-law buying stamps at the supermarket, they would be there, cameras rolling and microphones out, ready to ask some kind of quirky question about *Little Shop of Horrors*.

Fortunately for them, a think tank deep in the bowels of Seattle put their brains together and figured out a way to invent a celebrity magnet that opens way before the clubs do. In case the high price tags on scones weren't enough of a clue that the target clientele were the rich and famous, they decided to really spell it out by naming the place with a compound of the words *star* and *bucks*. It was an idea that was just crazy enough to work.

"Hey sexy."

In walks Fabian, six foot one with chin length dreadlocks and skin like midnight underneath cargo pants and the loudest blend of yellow and pink that has ever seen the surface of a button up shirt. At first glance, people generally do a double take and don't know if they should point him out to their gay friends or if they should put on some Bob Marley and ask him for a special brownie. As it would turn out, neither is true.

On an official level, he's my lawyer. He comes from a long line of lawyers that seem to be genetically biased toward never ever losing cases. His family has represented my father's family for five generations now.

On a personal level, he's a bad influence. That's what I always told my parents at least. When they snuck me into the clubs, it was generally disguised as his girlfriend. He's always taken good care of me, though. At least the tabloids certainly think so.

On a public level, we're much closer than friends. *US Weekly* snagged a photo of me giving him a peck on the cheek and now reports us as dating, being all hot and heavy and all that. *InTouch* says we're one fight away from breaking up. *E! True Hollywood Story* seems to like implying that we're engaged because I'm secretly carrying his child. Mind you, they've been riding that horse for far longer than nine months now. But my personal favorite so far is the story unanimously accepted by *Star*, *Weekly World News*, and *The National Enquirer*: Fabian and I share a telepathic bond ever since the aliens abducted and examined us using the same anal probe.

The truth is that Fabian really is my

lawyer. He passed the bar right around the same time that my parents started encouraging/developing my delinquency, so they put him on retainer to handle my legal troubles, even though those troubles never came. He still comes in handy, though. He's a huge part of both the legal community and the party scene in town. As a result, he knows a lot of people and carries a lot of information about the whereabouts and plans of people that wouldn't look quite right if it were me trying to find out. And upon giving me this information, he generally feels compelled to advise me against using it the way he knows that I will. But he understands why I can't take that advice.

By the time I gesture for him to sit down, he already is. "What's up, Fabe?" I ask, using the nickname he's always hated.

"That's never going to grow on me," he says, eyes shooting death in my general direction at the sound of the name. "You might as well call me Ian like everyone else does."

"Naw, the tabloids call you Ian," I reply. "I like to pretend I don't know any of the people they write about."

He laughs at me and now he's giving me what he calls the *all-knowing* look. I call it the *know-it-all* look. "You like to pretend they're not talking about you."

He's right. I try to disassociate myself as much as possible from the girl in the headlines. The girls whose every kiss looks like an affair, every drink looks like a binge, and every dollar spent looks like an uncontrollable spending spree brought on by the uncontained grief felt over the death of my folks. I would change my name but that would just give them that much better of a story to tell.

"They're not talking about me," I say. "They're talking about the me they're interested in writing exciting stories about. That me is way cooler than I am."

"So people would think."

"Anyway, they're talking about you too." I had to throw it in.

"I've got a lovely lady waiting for me who would be very upset if any of that turned out to be real." He pauses to take a drink. "Speaking of which…"

He leaves me hanging for a minute to draw out the suspense in the moment. My eyebrows raise as I sip about five dollars' worth of my coffee.

"Yes?" I finally ask.

He chuckles. "The aforementioned lovely lady friend mentioned a party tonight that we will both be attending. She was thinking it would be pretty nice if you came along."

"You don't say?"

"I do," he nods.

I was hoping this conversation was heading in that direction. Of course, Fabian doesn't generally know how to be that subtle. I'd better make sure that he means what I think he does and isn't just trying to actually invite me to a party.

"Where do you suppose this little get together would be going on?" I ask.

"There's a penthouse downtown. I believe that a Mr. Riley Bailey resides at the address. Who knows? You might see a familiar face."

Maybe he does know how to be that subtle.

"Well," I reply with a sly smile, "I wouldn't want to disappoint the photogs. I guess I'll see you there."

His smile, on the other hand, fades. "Listen, Windy…"

I know what he's going to say. "Let me stop you right there, Fabe. We've been through this. You know why I have to do this."

The table falls silent as he pours sweetener into his already sugar coma inducing Frappuccino. He picks up a spoon and begins to stir. "I know, I know. You spent four years preparing for this, it's the right thing to do, blah blah blah. Your little blind date gone awry wasn't even two weeks ago. Are you sure you don't want to wait?"

"Strike while the iron's hot," I come back immediately. "That's what dad always said."

I mentioned my dad. That was a low blow for Fabian. The families have always been close and I just implied that he doesn't care. I feel bad, but I'm right. I know I am.

He nods slowly, avoiding my gaze. "You don't think this is a little crazy?"

"Come on, Fabe. It's not like I like it. It's not fun. But if I don't..."

He puts his hand up to stop me. "I know, I know. I'll guess I'll see you there?"

"I guess you will."

I stand to go, leaving enough of my coffee behind to finance a small Somalian village for a month, and head out the door. I've got a lot to plan in a short amount of time. And, unfortunately, I've got clothes to buy. God forbid I appear in the same dress in two separate tabloids.

Sometimes I think Fabian plans these things just specifically so that I'll have to buy a new outfit in order to get anything done. Granted, a party is probably going to make this a lot easier, but it also requires me to spend time surrounded by crowds of people who think they're cooler than penguins and wearing clothes made by people whose names I can't even pronounce, much less spell.

Things are different when you're a little girl. I loved tea parties. I did the whole set up with my stuffed animals guests with names like Princess Patch or Jasmine Wolfe. I'm not sure if my mom ever noticed or not, but the fact that my tea party guests were generally named after doctors and/or diseases probably should have tipped her off that my intended future wasn't supposed to have cameras in it. I think she was more concerned at the time with making sure I only used the Royal Albert for my guests and not the Doulton. She loved to watch me. She loved to see me play dress up.

Two

As I step off the elevator onto the top floor landing, the multicolored strobes shine from beyond the penthouse doors and illuminate the dress that I paid entirely too much for, especially considering that it only contains about a square foot of fabric and I'll almost definitely never wear it again after tonight.

Mom would be proud. It's a bit ironic, I suppose. When she was alive, she encouraged this sort of thing and I hated it. When she was alive, I refused to do it. Now I can't stop.

I can't deny that there's a certain rush to it. In a dress like this, there's no shortage of drinks appearing in my hand from any number of admirers. Not that there's anything too admirable about buying a drink for a girl at a party where all of the drinks are free. Still, taking shots with the Seventeen cover girl or dancing with the pretty boy lawyer who thanks his lucky stars to have somehow been invited to the money parade is nothing to dismiss.

Speaking of pretty boy lawyers, I run into Fabian pretty frequently during the night. He's pretty consistently toasted after sundown, and tonight is no exception. He takes pride in introducing me to people that I usually already know by saying things along the lines of, "This is by far the nicest guy I ever sued," or "This girl don't need me to represent her cause she can represent on her own."

Sadly, I'd have to say that neither one of those are the worst line I've heard from him. But in his defense, I'd be pretty well plastered in his position too, stuck in a room where half of the people are clients and the other half are the ones that they sued. Awkward, to say the least. Let him take the edge off.

My edge is about gone for the night. I need to get some air. I find my way out onto the enormous balcony looking out across the Los Angeles skyline and head straight for the railing.

Twenty stories looks like a hundred after putting down enough shots of tequila. I remember the urban legend about dropping a penny off of the Empire State Building and that same penny gaining enough speed and killing someone when it got to ground level. The truth ends up being that the crosswinds at that height just blow it back into the building. The penny ends up back on a ledge or going into somebody's window not too far down from where it started.

I find myself wondering if the same truth applies to all falling objects as I vomit over the edge of the balcony.

"You know that thing they say about all work and no play?" I hear a male voice coming from behind me. "I think it might go both ways."

"What?"

It's not the question that I meant to ask. I already know the answer to that one. He's clever but not that clever. What I was actually going for was: *Who are you and why are you talking to me?*

I'm glad those weren't the actual words that came out of my mouth, though. When I turn my head I see the man of the hour standing before me: Mr. Riley Bailey.

"Oh… It's you." Those actually were the words I was going for, but maybe I should have rethought them.

He laughs at me.

"Thanks for coming to my party," he says through a grin that tells me he's entirely too amused.

I groan.

"No really," he starts again and steps toward me. "They say at every party someone has to be that guy, or girl in this case, that ends up puking their guts out off the side of the building. Now I don't have to feel obligated to be that guy."

Okay, he's trying to be funny. I guess I'll stop groaning now. I brush the hair out of my face and put my hand out to shake his. He takes it.

"I'm Riley," he introduces himself.

"I know. Riley Bailey. Your name rhymes. I always liked that about you." He gives me that awkward look that tells me he wants to believe I'm quirky but really just thinks I'm drunk. "I'm Windy…"

"I know," he interrupts me. "Windswept Rohm. You have an adjective instead of a name. I always liked that about you. I guess both of our parents had a sense of humor."

"Mine were trying for social commentary, I think. You know, the effect of the world on a girl born with money and a name."

He smiles. "Judging by the headlines, I'd say they were probably psychic."

Now I'm smiling too. "Yeah, my favorite was always 'Windswept Is.'"

We start to share a chuckle but are interrupted by a dull roar inside the penthouse. Only a few seconds pass before the roar becomes a chant. It takes a moment to realize that the word on everyone's lips is *Serenade*.

"Well," Riley says with a sigh, "looks like the party can start now. Madame Serenade has arrived."

Madame Serenade is the current flavor of the month. In a town defined by magazine covers, she's the *Maxim* girl sleeping with *Vibe* after sampling the blow off of *Rolling Stone*'s coffee table. A couple of years ago she found herself at an after party locked in a closet with a CEO, and it apparently worked out pretty well because she ended up flashing her goods on whichever version of *MTV* it is that still plays music. And now here she is.

"Well, if the party is just now starting," I say to Riley while straightening my dress and steadying my gaze, "I'd better get myself cleaned up. The night is young and I apparently have a lot of vomiting left to do."

He smiles and stares into his drink. "The bathroom is on the other side of the posse. Good luck."

"Thanks."

I start to walk away when Riley speaks to stop me. "Hey, before you take off to some movie star's apartment tonight..." He pauses for a moment as if trying to find the words. He eventually settles on "Have a good night."

I fight back the smile and nod before I turn to the door and get ready to battle my way through the entourage. I take a deep breath and pull open the glass door to find the majority of the crowd still chanting. They're loud enough that it doesn't surprise me when I finally notice that the DJ has decided he must usher in the diva by playing one of her own songs. Not the latest single, but the debut. That's the one that's always a hit. Everybody knows *Baby One More Time*, but your average Joe can't remember most of what came after that until the lead-in single for the next album which, for most pop stars, sounds exactly like the original debut. Madame Serenade only has the one album but my guess is that the DJ has been doing this long enough to recognize the trends.

Almost anyone who designs a large building with public restrooms tends to put them dangerously close to the front door, so I've unfortunately got to push my way through a sea of people that are packed together like sardines just to get to where I'm going. Normally, wading through the sea isn't that horrible of an issue for me, but the amount of time it's taking me will force me to hear this entire song. If the alcohol hadn't done it, the endless repetition of *honey honey, shake yer, money money, maker* would be enough to make me vomit.

I finally make it to the bathroom and the first thing I notice is that the floor is slippery. I'm apparently not the first one tonight to drink a little more than the stomach can take, and the housekeeping staff is on the spot. Of course, they could have mopped up the water a little more thoroughly or at least put down a wet floor sign, but they didn't. Predictable, isn't it?

There are three stalls in here. It's definitely not the corporate pirate's penthouse with one bathroom featuring his and hers everything and a bathtub big enough to fit six people, like you see Julia Roberts and Richard Gere sitting in when you watch *Pretty Woman*. Yeah, I'm sure there's one of those too, but for the guests there are separate men's and ladies' rooms. It's definitely a party suite.

Slipping and sliding across the floor, I

make my way into one of the stalls and spit into the toilet. When I'm done there, I hit the row of sinks and pull a toothbrush from my purse. As soon as I'm finished freshening my breath, I get started on touching up my makeup.

Touching up...
Touching up...
Killing time...
Touching up...

The touch up/kill time connection has been a staple in my social life since day one. My fourteenth birthday party was chock full of guests that I loved to see on television or listen to on the radio but didn't have the first thing in common with when I actually met them. I guess that was kind of the point. My mom and dad supported my goals from the start. I'll never doubt the support. But I also know that they were doing everything they could to offer me a safety net. Years of sending teenage me with a fake ID to every party that every name attended was a sure fire way to make a future for me should I fail or drop out on my way to curing cancer or protecting the innocent or inventing aluminum siding that really does look like wood. If I pressed the right flesh now, it may come in handy later. But after shaking hands with the guy who owns this and dancing with the kid who was sure to buy it from him soon, it was time to touch up. I can only take so much social networking before I needed to escape and spend an hour or two in the bathroom hiding and touching up...

Killing time...

Touching up...

Three

I'm certainly killing time right now, but I'm not hiding. Most of what I do is finding the appropriate spot and waiting for people to come to me. And people come. Lots of people.

Drugs and alcohol mixed with a lot of motion and body heat and a DJ who pounds bass lines straight through your temples leads to a lot of people doing exactly what I was doing on the balcony. And so they come, and I occasionally hold their hair for them just so that they'll remember seeing me, and then I help them touch up. When they leave, I go back to touching up my own makeup as I wait for the next person to come along.

After only seventeen minutes and four sick girls, the door opens and I glance over the shoulder of my reflection to see Madame Serenade stumbling behind me toward the first stall. She spots me looking at her and stops dead in her tracks. She straightens up the best the can and looks my over-touched up reflection in the eye and manages to push out, though not very well, the slurred words, "You paparazzi, bitch?"

I want to laugh. Not just a snicker but a full on guffaw. It's pretty close to what I expected her to say, but the alcohol brings out her strange accent. I don't know if she's British or Jamaican or a hobo or who knows what. Maybe a combination of the three?

But my face stays straight and I answer in the only tone understandable to a rich bitch, which is, in fact, by also sounding like a rich bitch. "I was on the cover of *People* the day I was born."

She can't decide if she's stumped, satisfied, or nauseous. The truth is that all three are equally accurate, but her answer is sufficient to challenge the first, belittle the second, and more than likely dwarfed by her desire to qualm the third. In her glossy eyed state, she breaks out a smug grin and asks, "Where you been since then?" I can tell that she's very proud of herself.

The appropriate answer would be along the lines of *My parents left me more money than I could ever possibly figure out how to spend*. Those words actually come out as, "I have a really good agent. He says my break is coming soon."

Her attitude makes a complete turnaround to being all sympathetic which, through the liquor, just comes across as patronizing. "Don't worry, honey. You'll get your shot."

I force my best smile out and express my overly bubbly gratitude. "Thank you so much, Miss Serenade. That means a lot coming from you."

"Now," she says quite unsteadily, as if she's try to decide if her efforts are best spent trying to stand up or trying to keep her eyes open, "I've got to puke up the last three hours so that I can make room for the next three."

"Oh, you poor thing," I say in the most genuine sounding voice that I can summon. "Let me give you a hand."

I walk up behind the figure that stands crouched in the stall over the porcelain god and put my fingers to her temples to pull her hair back. "There there, honey," I say. "Just let it all out."

"Thank you so much," she slurs. "You're a darling."

"Oh, don't mention it," I reply. "What would you expect from your biggest fan?"

She pauses her flow of vomit just long

enough to turn her head slightly and lets out a confused sounding grunt.

"Oh yeah," I answer. "I've been watching you for a long time."

I twist her hair around my wrist a couple of times, cup my palm around the back of her skull, and push her forehead as hard as I can into the toilet seat.

And again.

And again.

And again and again.

She moans.

I go again.

She moans again.

The blows total at ten before she stops moaning, moving, breathing, and all of those other things that go with life.

She's definitely not one worth crying over. The girl that sleeps her way to the top and when she gets there immediately looks down upon all of her subjects... I don't enjoy doing it, but people like her make it a lot more bearable.

I haven't been in the bathroom for as long as I expected to be, but it's still too long to think my absence wouldn't be noticed. So I make my way back into the penthouse where the crowd has significantly dissipated.

I catch Fabian's glance as soon as the door closes behind me. His face sinks because he knows what I've done. She went in and I came out. He knows that Madame Serenade won't be coming back to the party.

The girl he's been dancing with notices that he's stopped and puts her hand on his face as her expression sinks too, though she really has no idea why either one of them is frowning. I can't miss a beat though, and I have to make sure he doesn't miss one on my behalf. A man in a monkey suit passes by with a tray carrying five shots of some multi-colored liquid and I waste no time reducing his load to two.

"Fabie baby!" I say as I dance toward him with the three shots in my hands. "It's a party! Let's turn that frown upside down."

His girl takes two of the shots from me and hands one to Fabian. "Yeah, Fabie baby. The night's still young." She leans closer. "Very young."

I shoot him a knowing look and a muffled laugh. "Let's go ahead and take this shot so I can leave you two alone."

Fabian snaps out of it and takes the shot from her hand. He holds it up with a smile and says, "To old friends," with his glass raised toward me. He turns his glass to the girl and finishes with, "and a night full of promise."

I laugh again before our glasses go bottoms up. Fabian has always understood the correlation between shots going down the throat and hands going up the skirt. I turn around to set my shot glass down on a random surface and by the time I turn back to them, they've got their tongues down each other's throats. I suppress my gag reflex, content in the knowledge that what I've just done is once again the last thing on his mind.

"She seems like a really nice girl," I yell to Fabian over the music, not sure if he's even paying attention since he's found a place to plant his face. "I bet your girlfriend is really going to like her."

You always know a good friend by the way you need to go to lengths and try extra hard to get them into trouble just for the hell of it. Imagine my surprise when I start to walk away and hear him yelling at me from behind, "Who do you think is gonna hold the camera?"

Gross. That's our dynamic, though. I try my hardest to screw up his sex life and he tries his hardest to make me lose my lunch by telling me about it. If I didn't know better, I might say we were siblings.

I disappear into a sea of semi-familiar faces. I know who most of them are and I'm sure that a solid number of them recognize me, but I don't think that the majority of the people in this suite really consider any of the others to be friends. The tabloid television will hear rumors of two people showing up at the same party or in the same club two nights in a row and instantly report a new friendship or relationship. The truth is that most of these people never see each other without a drink in their hands unless their paths cross on a movie set or at a photo shoot. They work together, they party together, but they don't know each other.

Nevertheless, as I pass someone that I've met here or there, or at least think I have, I give the obligatory nod or smile, sometimes a hug or a kiss on the cheek. By the time I reach the other side of the room I've seen more faces than I can count. More importantly, they've all seen me as well.

I come to a solid wall of people facing the other direction, which universally implies that on the other side of that wall there stands the only thing that can hold the interest of that many people: a bartender. They say there's an actual equation that will tell you whether or not the alcohol is free at a party based on the number of Tony Award winners attending. I've never been able to figure out how the two are connected, but it proves to be useful when you're trying to determine exactly how drunk a person might be. But at the end of the wall stands the gracious host, Mr. Riley Bailey, who does not appear to have the slightest buzz. He's the only brick in the wall that's facing away from the bartender. I work my way over to him and he smiles and waves when he sees me approaching.

I lean in close to his ear and say to him, "I never got to wish you a happy birthday."

He turns his face toward mine and gives me a look that's a cross between amused and confused and says, "That's good. It's not my birthday."

"I know," I tell him. "I just couldn't figure out why you would throw a party that you don't seem to be even slightly enjoying. So I made something up."

He smiles, stares down at his drink for a second, and explains, "It's actually a business meeting. I'm working."

I know I generally come off as cynical and sarcastic and like to think that I know it all, but he lost me. As I realize this, I'm sure the look on my face must be priceless, because Riley is trying to hold back laughter. I don't have to say it, but I do anyway. "I'm lost."

He points to a circle of couches where around fifteen people are sitting, some talking, some making out, some smoking cigars, and some smoking cigarettes that aren't exactly cigarettes. But I gather that the ones he's specifically referring to are a couple of middle aged guys, one of whom is leaning back with a martini in his hand and an intrigued look on his face. The other is turned to him with an equally interested look, talking and passionately waving his hands around.

One of these two men seems to enthusiastically trying to convince the other of something, and the other seems to like what he hears. If I didn't know better, I might guess that Mr. Enthusiasm was trying to win his friend's daughter's hand in marriage, and they were discussing the number of goats it would require to make the nuptials a reality. I suppose I don't actually know better. Los Angeles is a strange place.

"I'm sure you recognize Arthur Curtis?" Riley asks, gesturing to the man sitting more at ease.

I do. "Doesn't he direct all of those horrible slasher movies?

"Right," he confirms. "Except that before he got to them, they were *extra* horrible. The man is a genius that should be winning Oscars but the studio doesn't give him anything to work with. Instead they give him large piles of crap and he turns them into really pretty, shiny, stylish, large piles of crap."

I laugh. "Okay then. Piles of crap. Got it. So then I take it you're his biggest fan?"

"Not exactly," Riley smiles. He points to the other man. "The guy on the right? The one who looks way too excited? His name is Gerald Dorset. He's a writer, also very talented. But the best job he's been able to get so far is on the writing staff of some crappy teen drama on Nickelodeon. Not even *Victorious*. The one that's on after *Victorious*. Do you know what's on after *Victorious*?"

I shake my head, not actually knowing what *Victorious* is either.

"Yeah," he says slowly, "nobody else does either. But if the two of them were to ever work together…" He trails off as if expecting me to fill in the blanks.

"…they would render their agents useless?"

Riley's award winning smile returns to his face. "Their agents are useless already. The writer's agent can't attract him any attention because he hasn't done any significant work on his own yet. Arthur's made enough blockbusters that he can pick and choose any screenplay he wants to direct, but his agent keeps setting him up for the surefire big money."

The pieces that were slowly coming together just snapped into place. "But if they happened to meet by chance," I suggest, "Gerald can pitch his idea in a casual atmosphere without those pesky agents jamming up the works."

He nods. "And I make sure the chance meeting isn't simply left to chance."

"So this entire party, with half the celebrities in the world attending, is all about making sure these two can be the show that's on before *Victorious*?"

He nods again. "And when the movie gets made, fifty percent of Gerald's initial paycheck comes to me."

My jaw drops. "Fifty percent? He agreed to that? You didn't ask him while he was puking off a balcony, did you?"

Riley laughs. "Believe it or not, not all of my guests do that. Mostly just you. No, Gerald still keeps all of his royalties. Fifty percent of one script isn't that much in the long run, especially considering the investment that he's making."

"Investment?"

"If just one of his screenplays gets made into a summer blockbuster film directed by Arthur Curtis, Gerald will never have trouble selling another script for the rest of his life."

Just as the last words come out, the music stops and it's immediately obvious that there's something happening on the other side of the room next to the elevators. I hear low voices rumble through the crowd and talking about the police arriving. Riley goes straight to the bartender to get some kind of information. Most of their conversation is drowned out by the noise of the crowd, whose voices are steadily getting louder. The two words I can make out clearly are the two words I've been waiting to hear: *Serenade* and *dead*.

I guess someone has stumbled across my handiwork.

I was seventeen when I tried to run away. Well, the police used that term when my parents called them. The truth was that I was just trying to get out for a while after getting into a fight with my mom and dad. I had grabbed the car keys and said that I was leaving, and they assumed that I meant for good. I was so tired of the parties full of fake people. I wanted a night to myself, a night on the town without the desperate camera guys that wait by the doors at all of the ritzy places. So I got into the car and drove away. I didn't know where I was going. I didn't really have a destination. My only plan was to go somewhere that I wasn't expected to be. So I drove until I started to see parking lots with cars that were more than two years old. Places where the parking wasn't valet. I pulled into the first place I saw that had a neon sign advertising some local brand of beer. For a while I had a really good time. Creepy old men bought me drinks. I played pool with guys whose beards were so long that you couldn't tell if they were Amish or trying to get on tour with ZZ Top. But the fun died when my mom showed up at the door. Leave it to me to forget that all of the vehicles they owned had GPS locators installed in them. And she was not happy. At all. So we stepped outside and we had it out. And after close to an hour of screaming at each other, of her not caring and me not listening or me not caring and her not listening, when we finally got through to each other, when we finally saw eye to eye, I looked at her beautiful face and knew for the first time, through my whole heart, that she loved me. And by the time that I realized that someone was standing behind her and putting a hood over her face, there was someone else putting a hood over mine.

Four

I don't envy the police. They've got their hands on a nightmare of a crime scene at the moment. The sheer numbers are astounding.

200 people at the party means there are

200 possible witnesses and

200 possible suspects.

157 separate fingerprints on her person, only

23 of which really make a difference because

134 of them are from people groping her at

4 parties she attended previous to this one.

19 gentlemen from the LAPD are

100 percent certain that there is

0 chance that the murderer would have stuck around this long.

And so our presence is graced by a crime scene unit that is absolutely certain that they are wasting their time. Nevertheless, every last partygoer hangs around until they've given a formal statement that they have no idea whatsoever as to what's going on. For the most part, they've been working their way from the door to the bar, which means that I'm set to be one of the last they talk to.

The exception is Riley. As the owner of the penthouse and the host of the party, he was the first they spoke to. Since then, though, he's been kind enough to keep me company while the detectives gradually work their way toward my end of the room.

Don't get me wrong, I'm not naïve. I fully understand that a guy's willingness to provide moral support has an almost measurable correlation to the length of a girl's skirt. But since I have to be here, I won't turn away intelligent conversation to pass the time.

Riley is a little apprehensive about how this might affect his matchmaker business, but I actually think this will do quite well for him. It's a town where the wilder the party is, the hotter the guest list turns out to be. It's only a matter of weeks before he'll be arranging the career of the next cliché pop superstar. And then it will only be a week or two after that when the only people that remember the name of Madame Serenade are the d-list celebrities on VH1.

At the moment though, there are several people with badges that still know her name, and one of them is approaching me. The gruff, older looking detective holds his hand out to shake Riley's, addressing him first. "Mr. Bailey, I'm Detective Leonard. Thank you for being so cooperative with our investigation."

"If there's anything you need from me, just say it," Riley says, taking the detective's hand and shaking it. He finishes the handshake and turns toward me. "Detective, this is Windswept Rohm."

The detective holds his hand out toward me for a handshake and I respond by throwing my arms around him. He lets out a short laugh and reciprocates the hug. "Hi Windy."

I let him loose and back up to stand next to Riley again, glancing over and seeing the bewildered look on his face. He struggles for a moment to find words and eventually settles on "I gather you two know each other?"

"We've met a time or two," I say.

The detective gestures toward me and begins to explain. "Miss Rohm here has a crush on me. At least I assume that's why she insists on going to the kind of parties that turn out like this." He looks at Riley and quickly adds "No offense, I just know she came here hoping I would show up."

"It's true," I joke back. "I can't resist an old guy with a badge and a trench coat he borrowed from Columbo."

Jerry Leonard, the detective in question, is absolutely right. I've known him for about five years, and this is certainly not the first time we've met. He's a homicide detective working with the major crimes unit. I once asked him the difference between major crimes and homicide and the only answer he could give me was a shrug, a mumbled comment about reporters, and then a not so subtle change of subject. He's usually stuck on high profile victims, being one of the few Hollywood homicide detectives that can tread lightly, play the press, and still get things done. That's how we met, and now he's one of the few people left that I consider family.

"Listen, Windy, did you see anything? Anyone?" he asks.

"Not really," I shake my head. "I was partying for a couple of hours and then I hit the balcony for some air…"

"I saw some of that air splattered on the pavement on my way into the building," he interrupts.

I guess that answers that question.

"...and then I got some more air in the bathroom," I play off of his joke, "took a shot with Fabian Winston and his floozy of the night, and I've been with Mr. Bailey here since then."

"Can you confirm that, Mr. Bailey?"

Riley staggers for a moment. "Well, I don't know about the times or anything, but she was with me since before you guys showed up. And I talked to her on the balcony too."

Jerry draws a notepad from his coat pocket and jots something down. After a moment he says, "You know she was found in the bathroom, right?" I nod. "They're going to find your prints among the other thirty thousand then. Did you happen to see her in there?"

"I must've just missed her." I know he's a cop, but sometimes he lays it on kinda thick.

He shrugs. "Well, I guess that adds up. We had a couple of girls, saw you in there. They had you there a good ten minutes before time of death, though. Listen, if you kids wouldn't mind puttin' together a statement for me... You can drop it by any of these uniforms on your way out. I'd appreciate it."

"No problem, Jerry," I say. "Thanks for

coming, old man."

He smiles at me and squeezes my shoulder just before he turns to walk away. "Get home safe," he says.

"Detective," Riley calls after him.

Jerry turns and looks at Riley with an expression that reads along the lines of, 'Why didn't you say anything before I turned around the first time?'

"Do you have any ideas on how long this will take?"

"You mean figuring out who did this?" the detective asks. Riley nods. "Well, if I were Sherlock Holmes, I could look around the room for a few minutes and tell you who the killer is and how he or she takes their coffee, if they're left handed, etc. It's a little bit more complicated than that.

"We've got crime scene analysts, forensic pathologists, forensic psychologists, medical examiners, and that's not even counting the folks with badges and guns. Truth is, I need twelve people to agree on a Kleenex before I can use it to blow my nose.

"What makes it worse is you got yourself a party scene here. Altogether that means that every person who came through that door is a suspect, including yourself. Our killer is gonna be a real needle in a haystack. It's gonna take some time. Nothing to worry about though. I'm pretty good at finding needles. In the meantime, look at the bright side: your party is gonna be on the front page tomorrow. That means you're not gonna have any trouble getting laid in the foreseeable future."

And with that, Jerry turns around and walks away.

Riley is speechless for a minute until he finally says, "He's a real character, isn't he? Can I ask how you two know each other?"

I don't meet Riley's gaze as I consider my words but instead stare blankly off in Jerry's general direction. Finally I answer with, "A few years ago I was a material witness in one of his cases. Now I'm kinda stuck with him."

I can hear the gears turning in Riley's head as I watch his face get paler and paler. "Oh my god," he says. "I'm so sorry, Windy. I forgot who I was talking to. The thing with your mom…" He trails off.

"Yeah, the thing," I mutter. The silence is awkward for a moment. If there's anything worse than an awkward moment, it's the awkward silence that emphasizes it. "Look," I break it, "don't worry about it. I prefer people don't associate me with that person they see in the papers anyway."

Riley tries to contain a grin but fails. "You mean that person that goes to wild parties and throws up off of balconies?"

"Yeah, that's the one," I say. "What kind of person would even do something like that? No one I know. Sounds like trouble."

"A little trouble isn't always the worst thing in the world," Riley says. "I hear it builds character."

I hate lines. I think I'm supposed to be flattered but really I just feel like I'm on a bad episode of Dawson's Creek. "I'm just gonna give one of these fine officers my statement and get out of here. This night desperately needs to be over."

I turn to look for an officer and Riley stops me in my tracks with, "Can I buy you dinner?"

I turn back to him and see the eagerness in his eyes. I don't know what to say. "Sorry, I don't really date."

"Please," he asks. "One dinner. That's all I ask. Then you never have to see me again." Great. More lines stolen from teen dramas. He's really bad at this.

"So you didn't get enough of watching my dinner come up? Now you want the prequel?"

"Listen," he starts, "I enjoyed talking with you tonight. I thought I might enjoy talking to you tomorrow night too. This time without me doing business, without you vomiting all over, without someone dying, I hope."

Straightforward. Damn. "Okay," I answer, "but I can't guarantee that everyone lives."

The general consensus is that anticipation makes time go by more slowly. The antithesis to this theory is found in the realm of oxygen deprivation caused by a patchwork hood wrapped tightly around your face. When you're passing out a lot, time passes pretty quickly. My few waking moments were defined by muffled engine sounds and motion sickness, which really didn't go well with the oxygen situation. I was pressed against someone that I assumed was my mom and my shirt was wet with something salty smelling, which I would also assume came from my mom. I don't know how long the ride lasted. The lucid parts really did last forever, but there weren't many of them. When the engine noise finally stopped, we were ushered through a series of doors. Our captors never said a word, just a series of nudges, prods, and tugs. The rooms were warm, and the air felt clean, not stuffy or humid. A long line of cop shows led me to believe that kidnap victims were always kept in cold, clammy warehouses. This didn't feel like that at all. One last prod was followed by the sound of a door locking behind us. It was quiet with the exception of my mother's sobbing. I asked where we were, not expecting anyone to tell me, just fishing for the sign of another human being in the room. There was none. I weighed the pros and cons, and fear was toward the top of the list, but not outweighing my desire for a deep breath without the taste of fabric in my mouth. I set myself, ignored the feeling in the pit of my stomach, and took off my hood.

Five

I wake up with the taste of fruit punch flavored Gatorade in my mouth. I hate Gatorade. It tastes like sweat. Pumping electrolytes into your body is a damn good way to avoid hangovers, though, and God knows I've had worse flavors in my mouth. Like grape Gatorade.

I pull the covers off of my face and look out through the window above my head. If my internal sundial is right, it's somewhere in the neighborhood of ten o'clock. Not bad, considering I didn't leave the party-gone-awry until four.

I look over at the alarm clock. Nine fifty-two. I missed coffee with Fabian. I guess that's assuming that he even showed up, all things considered. In either case, I'm sure he'll be dropping by soon enough.

I need a shower. I can still smell vomit along with all of the other pleasant smells that go along with a party. Alcohol, sweat, cop… God I hate smelling like cop.

I roll out of bed and head toward the bathroom that adjoins my room, shedding the tank top and shorts that I call pajamas along the way. Even though I live in Southern California where the choices in climate range from warm to warmer, there's still a world of wonder to be found in a hot shower. But as much as I'd like to just stand and let the water come down on me, I've got all of those aforementioned smells to wash away. And so I wash, scrub, lather, rinse, repeat, etc. and when I finally cut off the water I feel as though I didn't spend last night drinking and vomiting and killing divas and then drinking some more.

I wrap the towel around me and leave the bathroom, crossing the bedroom to my dresser. And though he doesn't think that I've noticed him, I'm fully aware that Fabian is sitting on the edge of my bed and staring at me.

"Some party last night," he says in an attempt to be nonchalant when he thinks he's going to startle me. And so I fake a startled jump so that he'll think that he really did sneak up on me. I suppose I've gotten into the habit of encouraging the overconfidence of others. It makes them feel good about themselves, and I never know when I'll be able to use it.

"No kidding," I say, pretending to catch my breath. "I hope my antics didn't get in the way of your little fling. She seemed really nice. And relatively disposable. I know you're into that sort of thing."

"It was a mistake," he says, not looking up and not missing a beat.

I sort through my dresser and find something to put on before answering. "Well, you make your own lifestyle choices. I try not to judge."

Clothes in hand, I make my way to the bathroom and close the door. I can hear Fabian's motion and assume that he stood to follow. "That actually worked out quite well," he says, the volume of his voice telling me that my assumption is correct. "No, I was referring to your lifestyle."

As soon as I finish dressing, I open the door and find Fabian standing right on the other side. "Yeah, I know what you're referring to," I say, trying to brush my wet hair and brush him aside all at once. "I'm not having this conversation right now. You know, I kind of assumed that if you so vehemently objected every time, you might not be so willing to participate. I appreciate your help. I do. But I really can do this without you."

"Yeah, I can see your judgment is impeccable. You missed the mark last night. Don't think I didn't notice."

He's completely right, even though he's entirely wrong at the same time. It does put a dash of perspective on the variety of facial expressions he was giving me last night though.

"She was on the list," I say. "How does that equate to missing anything?"

The look of frustration on his face is priceless. "You know damn well," he starts, "that she is not who you were there for. And you know damn well that I know that too. There is no way in hell you could've known she would show. Fuck, nobody in the world could have known. I'm pretty sure she didn't even know where she was after she got there."

I smirk as I put on my makeup. "You've been a lawyer too long," I say, teasing in nature but fully serious. "Everything has to be cut and dry. You forgot how to improvise.

"You're right. She wasn't the mark. The mark is relatively predictable. I know where to find him on a regular basis. In fact, I know where he'll be tonight. Serenade, on the other hand, is not only a diva but a hip-hop, pop princess, trendy, bar hopping diva. Like you said, *she* doesn't even know where she'll be showing up. I think that under the circumstances it was appropriate to make the best of the situation.

"Her second single flopped. Her fifteen minutes of fame are almost up. She was pissing her money away on parties. In about a week she would have fallen off the radar. I may have never gotten another chance like that."

"I hope you're right," Fabian says. He *knows* I'm right but he's playing coy anyway. "There's no room for error or experimentation when you're doing what you do. You plan this carefully. You wait for the right moment. You do it right. It works out." He pauses for a moment. "So how do you know where he'll be tonight?"

"He's picking me up at seven."

As soon as the words cross my lips, the look across his face is as if I'd just attached a pipe bomb to a rainbow colored school bus full of babies and puppies.

"You'll have to excuse me," he says. "For a second it sounded as though you were telling me you were dropped on your head as a child… over and over and over again."

I fight back a smile but eventually fail. It wasn't an original comeback, but it still amused me. "If at first you don't succeed..." I start and then trail off because the rest of that statement is implied.

He decides to finish my sentence with, "...you ask for advice from a retarded monkey? You have to know it's a mistake to be seen with this guy two nights in a row right before he dies. And you made plans with him? Real plans? Plans that he has a full day in advance with which to tell other people who he's going to be with?

"Your buddy Leonard seems pretty oblivious to the fact that people around you tend to drop like flies, but sooner or later someone will make a connection. And your recklessness is just making it easy for them."

"Don't think that didn't cross my mind," I come back with. "If I don't balance care and opportunity then I'll never be done with this. I know it's not necessarily the smartest move, but it's the one I have in front of me. If I don't take this chance then it could be months before I have another. I don't want the rest of my life to be spent on this. I want to be done."

"Keep making stupid moves like this and you'll be done alright!" He's raising his voice now, so I just stop talking. The room is quiet for a few moments. When he speaks again, his voice is calm. "You know, you could be done now. You could just go on a date with him, have a nice dinner, that's it. There's no law that says the night has to end in murder."

The conversations with Fabian always tend to come back around to this. And I know he's wrong but at times I'd really like to consider it. But I can't. I'm not going to leave unfinished business. I'm not going to leave this open. I can't. And I'm definitely not going to kill a heartless diva but stop when I get to the cute boy toy.

No favorites.

No preferences.

No emotions.

That's when I become a murderer.

Canopy bed. Window dressings. Color television. Really, REALLY nice furniture. My mom with a hood over her face. If it weren't for the latter, I might have thought that I was staying at the Four Seasons. That and the fact that the window dressings were posted on bare walls. She was still crying. I told her to take off her hood and as soon as she did I wished that she hadn't. The beauty queen with tears streaming down from bloodshot eyes through otherwise perfect makeup. My parents had always been the carefree stars of a fairytale life, and in that moment her eyes only showed me the collapse of the fable. As many times as I fought with the both of them over the concept of real life, for the first time I was very anxious to pretend that it didn't exist. I tried to make witty comments about our captors' excellent choice in décor. I would goof around and pretend to look out through the windows that weren't there, saying that I was sure I could see the Hollywood sign from our room. I even tried to find something good on TV. But the entire time, which seemed like forever, my mom just kind of stared off into nowhere. If she made any noise at all, it was sobbing. It went on like this for hours it seemed, until the door opened.

Six

The doorbell rings at 7:03 p.m. and, dressed very nicely if I do say so myself, I open the double doors to find an equally smartly dressed Mr. Bailey waiting on the step.

"Good evening, sir," I greet him with a slight bow of my head and a smile. "You're late. I'm afraid I've already made other plans."

"Is that so?" he smiles back. "I'm sorry to hear that."

"When you weren't here at exactly seven, I made arrangements to join a band of travelling circus folk and say goodbye to this town forever."

"Circus folk!" he stifles a laugh. "Are you joining one of their routines or supplying one of your own?"

In my most serious tone I answer, "The way I juggle rubber chickens is breathtaking."

He holds out his hand as an invitation for me to take is and says, "Then I guess we'd better be off before they arrive to steal you away."

And so we are.

The restaurant that he takes me to is a ritzy one that I honestly haven't been to since my parents brought me here on my twelfth birthday. Of course, when you're twelve years and going for an early dinner, the atmosphere is quite a bit different than you find in the evening. A scattering of overdressed families featuring somber faced children who would rather be at McDonald's or Chuck E. Cheese gives way to a dining room packed with what would loosely be referred to as *Hollywood's finest*. The emphasis is on the term 'loose.'

Young entrepreneurs with loose wallets are trying to impress perspective clients. Older entrepreneurs who, in most cases, can actually afford to have loose wallets are trying to impress beautiful women who are far too young for them. And those loose women are trying to make sure they wake up next to someone that can secure their lifestyle for the foreseeable future. And in the middle of it all a dance floor, where many of the aforementioned people will find their ways from point A to point B.

Though it's a full house with a line stretching out the door, Riley and I are seated almost as soon as the valet takes his car. I'm assuming that Riley did something particularly awesome for somebody that made that arrangement possible. Not much time passes before small talk ensues and in turn, light conversation inevitably becomes heavy as time passes and drinks flow.

"So are you a Hollywood native," I ask, "or were you carried here by a thousand angry drag queens?"

Riley chuckles. "You know, that's not too far from the truth. I kind of inherited the family business. My dad arranged meetings for a living as well. Of course, we were living on the east coast when he really got started, so his clients generally varied between Wall Street tycoons, union reps, and mob bosses. And unfortunately you can't take one without the others.

"So time went by and my dad inevitably got associated with some unsavory types that were strongly disliked by some other unsavory types. Some bricks flew through some windows. A few death threats were made. Long story short, he heard about a job on the west coast and we didn't hesitate in getting our bags packed. Never looked back. There's twice as much backstabbing out here, but far less of it is actual, literal backstabbing. That makes it a lot easier to stay clean."

I'm quiet for a moment, not quite sure how to respond. I settle on, "So where do the drag queens come in?"

Riley tries to hold back a smile as he explains, "You've obviously never met my father."

That makes me laugh and my laughing makes him laugh. A couple more drinks go down and a few minutes of small talk before he finally asks me, "So what's your story?"

"You know," I say, pausing for a moment, "you really don't have to do the whole first date 'where you from' routine. You already know my story. Everyone who's been awake at any point during the last five years knows my story. Born with a silver spoon in my mouth, tragically orphaned as a teen, constantly trying to commit suicide by way of alcohol poisoning... I'm sure there's a hall of fame somewhere that features matching party girl shrines of Paris Hilton and Lindsay Lohan. I'd really like to earn my spot in that hall."

"Yeah, I think I picked up something along those lines between the L.A. Times and Extra. I just get the feeling that your version might hold a bit more water. Barbara Walters has always seemed a little full of herself, you know? Kinda judgy."

He's right. I've seen enough to know that even if I hadn't made a spectacle of myself, even if I had been an upright citizen, the media would have found a way to crucify me. I don't like telling 'my story.' I'd rather just tell Riley to go fuck himself, walk out, and then *actually* run off with a travelling circus. On the other hand, it's a little refreshing to have a person that doesn't automatically assume that what he sees in print is the truth.

I take a deep breath. "Well," I begin, "my mom was a model named Kimberly Marks. My dad a real estate tycoon named Michael Rohm. They both enjoyed some moderate success in their respective fields, and it wasn't too long before they met at the sort of get together that young, successful people in Los Angeles might attend."

He interrupts with a snicker under his breath. "I think you already made my point," he says. "'Moderately successful?' It was almost like Cindy Crawford and Donald Trump were getting married, and you manage to be modest about it. Barbara Walters was totally off about you the whole time!"

I look at him with a smirk. "Are you telling this story or am I?" He shrugs in defeat and gestures for me to continue. So I do. "Alright, where was I? That's right... Donald and Cindy get married in a huge fairy tale wedding without a single photographer present and live a glitzy life, their names on the lips of every gossip columnist, until one day Cindy discovers that she's pregnant.

"They basically dropped off of the radar. Mom was collecting royalties off of every photo, movie, work-out video... basically everything she ever did. Dad had enough in the bank to live comfortably off the interest, and owned enough businesses and stocks on top of that. They made an appearance here and there but were in a position to never have to work another day in their lives. So they didn't.

"I was born and grew up with two stay-at-home parents. We lived a nice, quiet life until I was twelve. Then my parents had a nice long talk one day and decided that it was time for me to become a social butterfly, much to my chagrin. They had this idea that the only way I would ever meet a nice boy would be if they threw a party for me every Friday night and then snuck me into a club every Saturday night.

"I fought it every step of the way. I had aspirations of curing cancer, defending the innocent, building a bigger and better breadbox, something along those lines. So my seventeenth birthday comes, I'm getting ready to leave for Harvard, and my mother and father decide that their days to marry me off are numbered, so they need to redouble their efforts to get me into trouble. One night I've finally had enough and I walk out. My mom tracks me down, ironically, to a bar. She pulled me out into the parking lot and we fought it out. As we yelled and pointed fingers under the light of the neon beer signs, we were abducted."

I stop talking and look up from the silverware I've been fidgeting with to see Riley doing his own fidgeting on the other side of the table. He makes eye contact for a moment and then looks away.

He opens his mouth to say something but ends up closing it just as quickly when he realizes that he has no idea what he would say if he could bring himself to say it. Eventually I decide that his torture has lasted long enough and I continue.

"There are a lot of grisly details but the short version is that I made it out in one piece." I take another pause and fidget a bit more. The next words never get any easier no matter how much time passes or how many times I say them. "My mom didn't."

"I'm sorry," Riley interrupts me. "You don't have to do this. I know it can't be easy."

I consider his words for a moment. It's not easy. But life isn't easy. I need to finish.

"It actually feels good to talk to someone that's not just intending to put my words into a seedy newspaper."

A smile creeps across Riley's face that lets me know a bad joke is on the way. He doesn't disappoint. "So... does that mean I should turn off my tape recorder?"

I roll my eyes. The temptation for a comeback is almost overwhelming, and it would be so easy. But I want this story to be over so I trudge on.

"So at this point, the only family I really had left was Fabian. But in the next few weeks, Detective Leonard and I spent so much time going over statements, mug shots, and everything else that he got attached to this poor orphaned teenager. The guy practically adopted me."

"What about your dad?" Riley asks.

Another question warranting a hearty *fuck*

you response.

"When I came home," I answer, taking a deep breath, "my dad locked himself in the bathroom. For two weeks he only came out to eat once a day, and that was only with me pounding on the door. Day fifteen, I banged on the door and he didn't come out. I let it go for a bit, but eventually I needed to check on him. I found him in the bathtub with his face underwater. He had drowned himself."

Riley is quiet for another minute. I feel a little bad for him, even knowing that he's sitting right across the table feeling sorry for me. I'm not breaking the awkward silence again. I'm done talking. It's his own damn fault for asking.

"So," he finally clears his throat and starts to talk, "I know your detective friend. Who's Fabian?"

...

Odd is the only word I can think of to describe my thoughts at the moment. "Huh," I say. "It seems like you would know a guy before you would ask him to come to your party."

Riley seems to be shocked. "Oh, he was there?" he asks. "Was he that Jamaican looking guy you were talking to?"

"Oh, I take it you were watching me?"

He lets out a short but nervous laugh. "Yeah, I know. I'm creepy that way. Look, I totally hired a planner for the party. I only invited the two people that I wanted to meet each other. Everyone else was just background noise."

"Oh really?" I say, being coy. "So I was just background noise?"

"You," he starts and then gives a short pause, "were a fringe benefit. Anyway, where did your invite come from?"

Good point.

"Fabian," I answer sheepishly. "He's about the closest thing I have to family. His family and mine go back forever. God, I swear he's the only lawyer I know who hits a party every night."

"It's a wonder he wins any cases," Riley says. "That's the sort of thing you'd expect to need sleep for. He does win cases, right?"

"You'd be surprised," I reply. "He's never lost a single one."

"How does he do it?" Riley asks. "What's his secret?"

"A balanced intake of expensive liquor and expensive coffee. He's got so much damn Patron and Starbucks constantly running through his veins that he's perpetually ballsy and relentless. It's a good combination for his line of work."

My evening is interrupted by a familiar looking flash that reminds me of the ever present reality of my life: I'm a celebrity because they won't ever let me be anything else.

"I think you'd better watch out," I tell Riley, gesturing to the photographers and trying to force a smile. "Tomorrow morning there will be stories about me cheating on Fabian because I'm carrying your child and running off with you."

"I guess I can live with that," Riley says. I think I'm supposed to blush or something, but all I can actually process at the moment is the desire to get away from the increasing number of flashes going off. Then Riley breathes the magic words: "Do you wanna get out of here?"

The obvious question follows from my lips. "And go where?"

Mom was gone. They took her. I don't know where they took her, but they took her. Two guys had come to the door, and as soon as it opened she ran to them and fell to her knees, begging them to take her and to spare me. They looked like a combination of shocked and confused, but despite my screams of protest, they obliged to her wishes. I knew it was only a matter of time before they came back for me. I know it sounds horrible, but I prayed that they would rape her. I prayed that they would have their way with her and bring her back to me. In my mind, I figured that was the best case scenario. That was the only way I would ever see her again. In retrospect, I wish that had been the truth. I had been relatively calm up until this point. I had been calm for her. With her gone, I cried and prayed. I cried and prayed and made halfhearted attempts to think about how I would react if the door opened and she wasn't behind it. I thought of plans to storm toward whoever it was that came through the door and then... I didn't know what. I had travelled the entire way blindfolded. If I managed to make it out without being caught, God knows where the hell I would find myself when I opened the door. After feeling rebellious for the majority of my life, I just felt lost now. And so the door finally opened, and a shadowy figure that faced where I sat on the bed told me it was time to go. I did all that I could do. I did what I thought mom would do if I had gone and she were here. I looked up shyly at the man in the doorway and let out a slow, playful sigh. I stood and walked slowly over to him, raised my eyes to meet his, brought my fingers to his jawline and asked, "What does a girl have to do for a little leeway around here?"

Seven

At some point in my life, I may ride the elevator to the top of Riley's building without fully intending to decrease the surplus population before I come back down. Tonight is not that night. You'd never be able to tell, though.

Our hands are all over each other. Our lips are all over each other. If the elevator moved any slower, I think we'd be naked before it reached the top. Fortunately, the only thing on that floor is the penthouse suite owned by the one and only Riley Bailey.

The elevator doors open and Riley pushes me through the doors and up against the wall of the entryway as his lips move over every inch of my face and neck and mine against his. My eyes open just long enough to watch over his shoulder as the elevator doors close behind him.

The double doors to his penthouse, only seven feet away, seem like a mile from where we stand. My hand unfastens his belts almost simultaneously as his rides up underneath my dress.

"No," I say as he grips my thigh and pulls me even closer to him. "Not here. Not now."

And so he smiles as I wrap my legs around his waist. Our lips meet again and he carries me through the double doors. The room seems very strange when it's not filled with a million partygoers and/or cops. The enormous penthouse filled by only two souls, however horny they may be, seems almost tranquil. Almost.

I don't know if the doors closed behind us.

I don't care.

I should care.

I need to care.

I need to keep track of the variables. I need to eliminate variables. I need…

I need to take my dress off.

And so I do. It falls on the floor as he carries me toward where I assume there to be a bed. I need to keep track. I need to remember exactly where the dress fell.

I need his shirt off. And one button at a time, my need becomes reality. This is good. The less clothing for blood to spatter on, the easier it is to remove my trace. The less evidence that I was ever here. The less anyone will ever guess that he's dropping me on the bed right now and kissing me like I'm the last person he'll ever kiss.

I am the last person that he'll ever kiss.

I'm conflicted. Do I feel remorse? Pity? Guilt? Lust?

Oh fuck. It's lust.

His hand and now his lips are tracing every contour of my body. My fingers run through his hair and all I can think about is my hand on the other side of his zipper. I need control.

And so I pull his head up so his eyes meet mine. I push him onto his back and climb on top of him. I own him now. I can do what I want to do now. What I *need* to do now.

Even as he sits up and brings his face to meet mine, I know what has to come next. Even as he kisses me again. Even as his fingers run through my hair and down my back.

Even as...

Oh shit.

The shadowy man might have been attractive under different circumstances. But at that moment, as he leaned over me and I lay on the bed, I was less concerned about his looks and more concerned with the gun tucked into the back side of his belt. He tore off my shirt. I put my hands on his hips. He cupped my breasts. I grabbed his ass. He forced his lips against mine. I wrapped my fingers around the trigger and squeezed. And then he was grabbing his ass. His throbbing, bleeding ass. If the shot didn't attract attention, his screaming would, and so I took the gun in my hand and aimed it at his temple as his throbbing, bleeding mass shook on top of me. I risked the sound of another shot just to get him to stop screaming. I pushed him off of me. Tears ran down my face as I got off of the bed and ran through the still open door. I'd just shot and killed a man. I didn't know where my mom was. I was out of my pseudo hotel room, but I had no idea how to get out of the building. For that matter, I had no idea where the building was. This was the very first time I had ever even held a gun, much less fired one. Now it was my solace, my shelter, the only thing that made sense to me, made me feel secure, safe. And so I travelled through my insecure world outside of my Four Seasons prison, secure cold metal in my hand, searching for my mom's adjoining room.

Eight

I open my eyes to see the sun shining through Riley's gigantic windows, stretching from wall to wall, ceiling to floor. Sunrise is the only time that I'm ever impressed by the Los Angeles skyline. If you've seen one skyscraper, you've seen a million. But when those skyscrapers reflect the light from the morning sun, when they filter the rays from one set of windows through to the windows on the other side, the real sparkle of Hollywood is apparent, and you gain a whole new perspective on life. My perspective at the moment is that I fucked up pretty hard.

I sit straight up in the bed. The conflict is killing me. I know why I came here. I believe in why I came here. Now I'm having second thoughts. Now I'm thinking about Fabian's words. What am I doing? I came here to lure him into what he had coming. I let myself get lost.

I swing my legs over the side of the bed and stand up. Riley is still asleep or else he would get a pretty decent view of a fully nude sun drenched Windswept picking his shirt up off the floor and putting it on.

It's funny how a room will look different to you according to every different situation you find yourself in. The first time I was here, it felt like a club, shoulder to shoulder with people drinking and dancing. Later that night if felt like a refugee shelter, full of people waiting for the next move after what they considered to be a tragedy. Last night it was a blur of destinations, where every detail was meaningless if it didn't facilitate the two of us getting closer to the bed. Now, in the morning light full of new perspectives, it is devoid of agendas. And so I take it in just as it is, with no thought of what use its various aspects could be to me.

I leave the bedroom, whose only occupants are a dresser, a wardrobe, and a king size bed supporting a still unconscious Mr. Bailey. The main room lies beyond, featuring a bar, a ring of sofas, and a hardwood floor, still clear enough to support the club like dancing scene from two nights past. Of course, the only one of these features that interests me right now is the bar. My night certainly didn't end up the way I had planned.

I make my way around the bar and locate the necessary elements for a vodka and coke. It's not exactly coffee, but given the situation I've placed myself in, coffee won't exactly meet my needs at the moment. And so I continue my exploration of the penthouse, drink in hand, and make my way to the door opposite the bedroom.

Judging by the desk covered in sheets of paper and the bookshelf featuring nothing but composition books, I would guess that this is Riley's version of an office. The corner of the desk holds a loosely mounted telescope, and it makes me wonder if he uses it to check out the paparazzi that must certainly be staring back at him through the gigantic glass panes on a regular basis. I'm sure they've gotten some great photos of me over the last two nights.

I circle the desk and sit down in the chair behind it, thinking of what kind of meetings Riley must arrange and what parties he plans around them while sitting in the same chair. I wonder which of my favorite movies were only made because of a call that came in through the cell phone that sits in front of me on this desk.

"For a minute, I thought you ducked out

in the middle of the night."

I look up with a start at the sound of Riley's voice. He's standing in the doorway with that grin he gets after he thinks he's said something witty and/or charming. I smile back.

"I would never just take off like that," I say. "That dress on your floor was way too expensive to leave behind."

He chuckles as he walks toward me. "So what are you up to so early today?"

"Just snooping around through your most private of secrets," I answer. "I'm sure you must have a good recipe for peanut brittle in here somewhere."

He reaches the desk, picks up my drink and smells it. "Oh my god," he says with a disgusted look on his face. "The headlines must be true. It's barely sunrise and you're already hitting the hard stuff. It's amazing you stay awake long enough to have so many late nights."

I lean back in his chair and give him a sly, playful smile. "I've heard you have a shady past. A girl has to be ready for anything."

"Oh, I see," he replies. "Well? Find anything incriminating?"

"Well," I look back at him, "I've noticed that the only room you have on your bookshelf is for things that you wrote. You seem to be guilty of severe egotism. And I've got about seven thousand composition books as evidence."

He laughs. "You caught me," he confesses. "My words are more important to me than anyone else's. I'm the only one I can guarantee isn't feeding me bullshit."

My witty comeback in this witty banter is interrupted as Riley's cell phone, laying on the desk in front of me, begins to ring. Playfully, I pick it up and answer, "Mr. Bailey's office."

The phone is quiet for a moment with only a very faint, shallow breath on the other end until a click brings the phone call to a close.

"Who is it?" Riley asks me.

An awkward smile crosses my face. "I guess they didn't want to talk to me," I joke. "They hung up." I put the phone down on his desk and stand from his chair. As I walk around the corners to face him, I say. "I would have told them that you were in a very important meeting anyway, and couldn't possibly be interrupted."

"Is that so?" Riley replies, putting his hands on my hips and looking into my eyes.

"Oh definitely," I reply, leaning forward to kiss him, if only for a moment. "I've got you booked all morning."

We kiss again.

…and again.

…and again.

We finally let loose of each other and I make a clever comment to fill the conversation, even though I'm only really intending to make space before another kiss.

I pick up the phone and start to speak, "I guess you'll just have to return a call to…" I read the *one missed call* message on Riley's phone, "Fabian?"

A thousand thoughts race through my head.

Is this the same Fabian? It can't be the same Fabian. What had Riley said last night? 'Who's Fabian?' and 'Oh, was he there?' And then it hits me all at once. I'm so stupid. I let myself forget why I came here. I let myself like him. Worse than that, I let myself trust him.

Still leaning against the desk, I inch away from Riley along the edge of the desktop, feeling its corners and the telescope turning on its mount behind my back as I move across it.

The smile fades from Riley's face. "What's wrong?"

Before I can answer, I move past the corner of the desk and fall back onto the floor. I land on my ass but my eyes never leave Riley's.

He rushes over to where I've fallen. "Are you okay?"

I don't think before this moment I've ever fully grasped the concept of *seeing red*. But as I feel my rage build, I focus on the object of that rage leaning over me, extending his hand toward me, ready to expand on whatever lies he had already been telling me.

At this moment, I need to say something but I can only bring one word to my lips. The same word that I read only moments ago. The word that turned my world inside out:

"Fabian."

And just as my world fell apart at the moment I realized there was a secret between the man I just slept with and the only person I trust, I watch as the look on Riley's face tells me that he's coming to the realization that I've caught on, even if he's doing it at the lightning fast speed of a retarded monkey. His lips turn to jello and his eyes turn blank as I see him struggling to find any kind of words to fit the situation. And then, as if on cue, he speaks the three words that he thinks will make things alright. The three words that will assure me that nothing is alright at all.

He says, "I can explain."

That's what I needed to hear.

I roll onto my back and with the same motion, my leg swings up. He shies away just far enough to bring his head up to the appropriate level that when my foot hits the telescope that peeks over the edge of the desk, it spins around and makes contact with his face. I don't think he's even remotely hurt or even stunned, but it forced him to stumble back to the point where I can plant my feet on his chest and push him away.

With only a couple of feet between us and only a moment to gain any ground, I roll back toward Riley, ripping the telescope from its mount along the way, and push him to the floor. I straddle him, putting the telescope across his neck and bringing my face within inches of his. Our eyes meet, and for a moment I wonder if I stare hard enough, I may not have to ask anything. My gaze might just penetrate his soul.

I'm not that patient.

"I've got a three inch refractor pressed down just hard enough that you should be seeing stars," I say, feeling entirely too pleased with my pun given the situation at hand. Focus. He needs to talk. And so I put my lips less than an inch from his gasping mouth and I breathe the word once more: "Fabian."

"What the fuck?" Riley chokes out. "He didn't want me to say anything." I glare at him, waiting for him to give me something more useful. "He asked me to find him some clients. Business is slow. He didn't..."

Riley's sentence is cut short as I push down on the scope. "Listen, Riley," I grit my teeth, "last night happened because I wanted it to, not because of my inability to see through your lines. I don't speak bullshit, so let's move along now."

I feel him try to push me off of him, but he can't find the breath. He's eventually still and forces his gaze to meet mine. He coughs briefly before letting out a resigned, "Okay."

I push myself up and put the telescope back onto its mount. Riley gets to his feet, rubbing his throat along the way. He walks around the desk and sits in his chair. He takes a sip from my drink and then we're both quiet for a moment, me waiting for him to talk and him deciding what to say.

When I decide that the moment has lasted too long, I take the opportunity to remind him just what it is that I want to hear about. "Fabian."

He glares at me for a moment. "Yeah," he finally says, "Fabian."

We stare at each other for another moment. I'm on the verge of picking the telescope up again when he finally begins to speak.

"I wasn't entirely truthful about my father last night," is how he starts. "We came out here on honest business, but the business didn't stay honest. I've managed to find a niche between actors, directors, writers... whatever to keep afloat. Dad wasn't able to find that niche. So he fell back in with the unsavories.

"It's a different brand of crook out here. Any time you may have been told that Hollywood is dirty... you haven't heard the half of it. Money buys quite literally anything, and there are an endless number of people with the money to spend. The tycoons in New York want crack. Here they want it from some exotic location. The cigars have to be Cuban. There's no jewelry but blood diamonds.

"I'm sure you've heard of people with enough money to buy and sell whatever or whoever they want? Here they don't have to buy the whole person. Just the parts that they want."

I was on the verge of a panic attack. Granted, I probably should have panicked long before, but I was forcing myself to be focused, just as I had forced myself to be calm for my mom. I needed to be calm now. I needed to find her and get out. There would be time to break down later. There would be time when we were safe. But the panic was pounding at the gates. I wandered strange, dark hallways, in a strange, dark building, wondering how long it would be until someone found me. Someone had to have heard the gunshot. It felt like hours since I had escaped my room, though I knew it couldn't have been more than a few minutes. Just the same, someone must have known I was gone by then. I looked into every room I passed, half hoping to see no one at all. No one that would be looking for me, trying to kill me. The latter half of my hopes were realized, as no one inhabited any room that I entered. It was almost as though they had all left when they heard me coming. Maybe they had. All of my hopes were draining as I began to hear the sounds of wind and knew I was nearing the exit but still I had no mom. I came to one last door and pushed it open to find the last thing I ever wanted to see. It was my mom. It was what was left of my mom. She laid there on the floor, naked, blood flowing from what seemed like a thousand precise cuts. I knew I would feel nothing but I checked for a pulse just the same. My efforts to be calm failed me. I collapsed on her hollow body and began to sob uncontrollably.

Nine

"He tried to contain it," Riley says, as if in an attempt to explain away his father's actions. "In New York he would do anything for a buck regardless of who it affected, until it started to affect his family. We came out here and he tried to contain it. He couldn't keep his hands completely clean, but he wanted to at least keep from hurting anyone.

"But I did get hurt. It wasn't by anything he did. It was a random drive by. A bunch of assholes just trying to get initiated into some gang. Just the same, it put me on a machine. He's trying his damnedest to make sure nobody gets hurt because of him, and I'm still sitting in the hospital with a tube down my throat because my lungs aren't gonna work on their own.

"Obviously, my dad's line of work doesn't offer benefits, and lungs aren't cheap. So he did what he does best. He introduced some people with organs to some people with money and took my lung as payment."

Haphazard pieces have danced around my head for years now. Long enough that I've learned to ignore them. Now they're falling into place at such an alarming rate that I'm not sure whether everything is coming together or if it's going to shatter everything I thought I knew.

Or both.

"Fabian is the people with money."

Riley glares at me with a look that's conflicted between knowing he has all the answers and wishing that he didn't. "Fabian knows a lot of people with a lot of money. My dad claimed a lung and Fabian arranged buyers for the rest."

I fight back tears. I'm getting emotional. I can't get emotional. I summon all of my rage and manage to channel it into a murderous glare aimed straight at Riley. I don't have to say it but I do so anyway. "My mom was *the rest*."

I can tell that he's weighing what his next move should be. "I know it doesn't bring your mom back, and I'm sure it sounds hollow, but I'm sorry that my dad did what he did. I'm sorry that she died so that I could live."

I let out a short but loud laugh. "You make

it sound as though it was her choice!"

"I know. I know. Look," he starts as he opens a drawer in his desk, "Fabian told me to be ready for you."

That bastard.

Riley pulls a small revolver from the desk drawer and continues. "He said I should expect you to try and exact some kind of revenge on me for what my father did."

I don't respond. I make no gesture, show no reaction, save my eyes watching the gun as he pushes the shells into it one by one.

"I've only known you a short time, but in that time I've seen more depth and understanding in you than Fabian gives you credit for."

He sets the gun down on the desk.

"I don't think you want to kill me. I think you're deeper than revenge."

My eyes move between his face and the fully loaded revolver that lies between us. What's his game?

"Take it," he gestures toward the gun.

I don't trust him at all, but if there is a loaded weapon in the room then I think I should be the one holding it. And so I take it. I don't point it at him, but his eyes still grow wide. He takes a deep breath and swallows, as if trying to build up his nerve. Finally he stands up, hands at his sides, and looks straight into my eyes.

"Alright, Windy," he starts, "do it. If you're so damn bent on revenge, so desperate to avenge her, pull the damn trigger. I'm ready. Just fucking do it."

I point the gun at him for just a moment, watch as his pulse builds so high that his throat is visibly trembling, and then lower the gun. I stare at the cold metal in my hand and say, "I'm not interested in revenge."

Riley lets out a breath so heavy that you'd think he'd been holding it for a year. He puts his hand on his chest as if checking to make sure his heart still works, and collapses back into the chair. After a moment, he looks at me and says, "I really thought that you were gonna do it."

I swallow. "You're a good guy, Riley."

His look turns to one of sympathy. "I'm sure it's no consolation," he starts (and I might add that that's the worst possible way to start a sentence), "but her sacrifice did save my life. And in a way, your mother lives on inside of me."

All I can do is shake my head. "There's only one problem," I tell him, lifting my gaze to meet his. "It doesn't belong to you."

By the time Riley realizes that I've raised the revolver's barrel to be level with his chest, the hammer is already falling.

I'm not worried about the sound of the shot. With the kinds of parties that Riley held, this has to be the most soundproof room in the world. The sound that concerns me is the one that has just begun to come from Riley's phone. I lean over the desk and stare down at the screen that is once again displaying the name of Fabian Winston. This time it's a text message.

I pick the phone up and press the appropriate key to bring up the message that reads, "Did you take care of it?"

Riley was supposed to kill me. Two people I had let myself trust had a secret between them, and now I'm in on it. I'm a loose end to tie up.

I've known Fabian for my entire life. It would be rude not to reply.

I key in the words, "It's done," and press *Send*.

I was unhinged. Mom was gone, her lifeless body underneath mine as I leaned over her and cried. When we arrived in our ritzy prison, I had tried to be the strong one. I had tried to calm her down. Convince her we would make it through. But nothing was alright. I blamed myself. I killed her. If I hadn't run away, they couldn't have taken us from the bar. I shouldn't have told her it would be alright. I should have tried to figure out a way to freedom sooner. Freedom? What was I talking about? I still didn't know where the hell I was or how to get out. That's what I needed to do. I needed to get out and get help. The building felt pretty empty save myself, the man I left in the other room, and the woman I shared this room with. Still, if there were someone else there, my mom would never forgive me if she died and I stuck around and let the same thing happen to me. I needed to get out, get to the police. If they identified the man I killed, they might get the rest of them. I killed a man. I couldn't believe I killed a man. I needed to get out. I didn't want to leave my mom. I felt like I had already hurt her so much and now I would be abandoning her one last time. But I needed to get out. I needed to get help. So I squeezed her hand, kissed her forehead and I left her right where she was.

Ten

I left Riley right where he was. If his walls
and floor are thick enough to hold in the sound,
I'm sure that they'll be able to keep the smell in
just fine for a while. At the moment I've got
something more urgent to focus on: Fabian.

He thinks I'm dead. I need to find him
before he discovers otherwise. It's still semi-early,
so I'm guessing he'll be at Starbucks. A logical
person would maintain his routine so as to not let
on that he knows I'm dead. Fabian just wants his
Starbucks. Hollow and status driven as it is, it's
just good shit.

So here I am, caffeine and whipped cream
deprived, pulling up to the building that houses
Fabian's law firm in Riley's Aston Martin. I park
in the lot, knowing that the valet would just tell
Fabian that I'm here.

My adrenaline is killing me. Time seems
surreal. I make my way from the car, across the

parking lot, through the lobby, and up the stairs in what seems like only seconds. As the elevator doors slide open in front of me onto Fabian's floor, I'm certain that I can literally feel time slowing back to normal rates.

I stroll up to the receptionist's desk, calm, confident and smiling and prepare to lay it on as thick as possible.

"Windy!" is what I'm greeted with. "I haven't seen you in weeks! Is Mr. Winston expecting you?"

I smile at her. Julia is a sweet little old lady that's been helping out Fabian's family for decades, since before I was even born. She's such a dear. I'll have to make sure that whatever happens, she's not here for it.

"Oh no, Julia. I was hoping to surprise him. Do you mind if I wait in his office?"

She smiles back at me. "Go on in, dear. He should be here soon."

"Thanks so much," I say as I open the door to the left of her desk leading to the hallway lined with lawyer's offices. "Don't tell him I'm here, okay?" I see her playfully put her finger up to her lips in a *shush* motion before I disappear through the door.

I make my way toward Fabian's office

which, on a regular basis, is the only one occupied. The six doors that I pass on the way lead only to rooms that are empty with generally only a desk and a chair or two to fill them. I think Fabian bought a large office solely for the purpose of being able to say that he owns a large office. He insists that he keeps the extra rooms for other lawyers to use when he's collaborating with someone else on the same case. I'm ninety nine percent sure that he regularly cites the size of his office in the process of getting laid.

In either case, Fabian is going to have some explaining to do very shortly, and I get the feeling that he won't be worrying too much about girls or lawyers after that. And now, as I reach his office and close the door behind me, the only thought that worries me is the question of why.

I think the average person would have about a million questions and/or reasons to not believe that their best friend was capable of such a thing. That's not me. Fabian comes from a long line of fine gentlemen that have always been quite talented at putting money into their pockets. There isn't a single act that I would put past that family. He may claim to feel bad, but he doesn't feel bad enough to stop.

But why her? I stand behind his door with

Riley's revolver in my hand, waiting to ask him just that.

I can feel time slow down again as a few minutes begin to feel like an hour. But my patience or lack thereof becomes a non-issue as I hear footsteps coming up the hallway toward me. I close my eyes and listen as they grow louder, drawing near. Time gets slower and slower. My heart beats faster and faster. I try to slow it by focusing on his footsteps, counting them, pacing my heartbeat. I'm not going to get any use out of adrenaline. I need a clear and level head. I need to think straight.

In the course of less than a second, three things happen:

1) The door opens.
2) The barrel of the revolver becomes one with Fabian's left nostril.
3) My level head takes a very heavy tilt.

"Get inside," I breathe, barely above a whisper. "Close the door."

Fabian wasn't expecting to see anyone. He sure as hell wasn't expecting to see me. "Windy," he begins to speak, the shock in his voice apparent. "I…"

I don't have the patience for this.

"Get inside," I say again, much more

slowly this time, "and close the door."

He inches toward me, head tilted back from the discomfort of the cold metal in his nose, and reaches behind his back to close the door. My eyes never leave his, and his eyes stay focused on my trigger finger.

I press the gun against his face hard enough to back him into a corner. I don't actually want him in the corner, but the aggressive symbolism was important for the moment. We stare at each other. I'm waiting for him to say something. Anything. I don't want to hear it, but I want him to try. He's scared. He doesn't know if he should cower or try to talk his way out of this.

The attorney in him takes over and his mouth opens. "Look, Windy, I…"

But I won't let him finish.

"Shut the fuck up!"

He cowers further into the corner. The look on his face would make me feel sorry for him under different circumstances, but at the moment it fills me with an odd satisfaction. The balance of the two levels my head again. My calm returns.

"Sit down behind your desk," I direct him, my eyes still fixed on his.

He keeps his back against the wall but

inches his way out of the corner toward the other side of the room where his desk sits. The barrel of the gun remains steady between my eye and his face as he finds his way awkwardly into his seat. I can trace every stage of his expression as he tries to regain composure. I know him. I own him.

"We can have a civilized conversation if you behave," I say. He doesn't respond so I continue. "Tell Julia she can go home early."

Fabian's eyes stay connected with mine as he presses the intercom button on his phone and begins to speak. "Julia," he says, "I've got a clear afternoon today. I'm just gonna hang with Windy for a while. Why don't you take off for the day?"

The silence that follows the end of his sentence as we wait to hear her voice is deafening, but she responds after only a moment. "Thank you, Mr. Winston," her reply rings through the speaker. "Now, you two don't hang out too hard. You've got meetings in the morning and we're almost out of Tylenol."

The room fills with silence and Fabian and I just stare at each other for another minute that feels like ten. "Your face is priceless," I finally say.

He considers for a moment before responding. "I'm not generally accustomed to walking into a room and having my nose picked with a Colt."

"You didn't expect that I'd still be breathing, did you?"

He's trying to plan his next words very carefully, though I'm sure not carefully enough. His mouth opens to speak a couple of times, but then it closes again. I'll make this easier for him.

"I can see that you're weighing this conversation in your head very carefully and you're not sure which approach to take. So let's talk this through.

"You know me better than anyone. You're practically family. You know me well enough to effectively lie to me, because you can fairly accurately predict what I'll believe and what I won't, and that creates a guideline for what to say to me and how to say it. When you add that to the point that you've been stringing me along for a few years now without arousing the slightest bit of suspicion, your confidence must be at a peak.

"On the other hand, you're processing the knowledge that I've had a very enlightening morning, and you're trying to decide what that will mean. What do I know? What would he have told me and what would he have kept to himself?

For that matter, what exactly did he know in the first place? Do you even have to worry about what I might know, outside of the personal ramifications?

"And then the million dollar question: You weren't at all expecting to see me. If I'm not dead, does that mean that Riley is? If so, what does that mean for you? I don't envy your position, Fabian. But maybe, just maybe, the truth will set you free."

He stares at me. He's been staring at me since I started talking. The look on his face tells me that everything I've said lines up with everything he's been thinking. He's trying to find somewhere in the depths of his imagination the one thing he could possibly say that might convince me to let him live.

"Windy," he starts, "I didn't know it was your mom."

That wasn't it.

"No?" I ask in a tone that lets him know I'm not buying it. "Did you start out not knowing or were there just enough dollar signs to make you forget?"

He shakes his head and looks away. "It wasn't like that."

Really? *Really?* I lose it. Before I realize

what I'm doing, I'm around the desk and looking down at him with the barrel of the gun pressed between his eyes.

"Then what the fuck was it like, Fabian?!" I'm screaming now. "What the *fuck* was it like?!"

He's shaking so violently now that when he tries to lean away from the gun, he falls over in his chair.

"You've got some kind of explanation for me, Fabian?" I ask, looking down at him. "Tell me what it was like!"

He's shaking still. He's trying to find the words. He stutters for a moment and finally manages to spit out two words: "Designer organs."

"Designer organs" are the words I heard from the detective's mouth as I sat shivering on the ground outside of the cold dark building I had just escaped. I could barely bring myself to speak, but when I did it was to ask why. Why us? Why this? The best he could give me was that we must have been spotted by someone in the organ business who jumped at the opportunity. I didn't understand. I thought it was my fault for running away, for leading my mom to the crappy bar in the middle of nowhere. He told me it wasn't. He said that none of it was my fault. Not the kidnapping, not what happened to my mom, and not the man in the building who lay dead by my hands. If it wasn't us, it would have been someone

else. At least I made it out. They could link the man I killed to known accomplices and shut them down now. He said I was a hero, and that didn't make me feel any better. My dad being on his way didn't make me feel any better. The detective promising that he would look after me didn't make me feel any better. Nothing did. My mom was gone.

Eleven

"Bailey came to me," Fabian starts. "He had a business proposition. He told me he had something to sell and it was something that my clients might be in the market for. I wasn't interested at first. It seemed like more trouble than it was worth, but then I started crunching numbers and figured out that it was going to be worth a hell of a lot more than I anticipated."

"You mean my *mom* was going to be worth a hell of a lot more than you anticipated."

"I didn't know it would be her," Fabian says abruptly. "Your boyfriend's dad didn't either. I had nothing to do with the harvesting, the planning, the distribution. There were a lot of people that played a lot of different parts. Mine was just to find people in need of a service that could afford to pay for it."

"Why did he need you?" I ask. "He knew his way around the black market, and how to find buyers. That's not exactly your forte."

Fabian pulls himself off of the floor and moves around the desk to the chair I had previously been sitting in. I let him go but keep the revolver trained on him as he sits down.

"Bailey wasn't interested in the black market," he starts again. "His concept was much bigger. He called it 'designer organs.' A person can find a black market heart in Los Angeles for under fifty thousand. Heart, kidney, lung, doesn't matter. But for someone who has enough money, how much would they pay for a heart from an actor? A kidney from a supermodel? How about a lung from your favorite author?"

"And I led my mom out into the open in a bad part of town," I say. "How could they resist a target so easy?"

So it really was my fault then? They were looking for a certain type of person and when she followed me that night, I made her a sitting duck.

As if answering my thoughts, Fabian leans toward me slightly and begins to speak. "I didn't know that your mom would be a target. I had no idea until after it was done. But it had nothing to do with you. These people planned very carefully and they knew what they wanted and who it was coming from. If you and your mom hadn't been in that parking lot, they would have done it somewhere else."

At some point since Fabian sat down, I had found myself leaning against the desk. Now, as he speaks, as I realize that my mom was marked for death long before I ever ran out, I find myself slowly sliding down its front surface until I'm sitting on the floor with my back to Fabian, because my legs just don't want to work anymore. My body goes limp. The gun drops between my feet.

"Up until that point, I actually managed to justify what I was doing. It wasn't even the dollar signs that made me think it was okay. I thought that if ten, even five people lived from the pieces taken out of one person… The math made sense. One life for five. It seemed right."

"And the price was right too?" I interrupt. My head begins to clear. When he says words like *justify* and *right*, my anger returns to remind me why I'm here. Why we're having this conversation. Why he's not justified and he's not right.

"I've always loved your family," Fabian says, rising from his chair and coming back around to my seat on the floor. He squats beside me. "Your mom wasn't the first, but she was the last. I told Bailey that I couldn't do it anymore after that. He would have to find his buyers elsewhere. It turned out to be a moot point.

"Your mom's left lung was a perfect match for Riley, so Bailey Sr. was out too. You escaped from their facility. The police knew where it was all of a sudden. There was a man in the department that Bailey had looking the other way. He advised us that the building would be linked to the harvesters and that if we didn't lay low, it would eventually link to us."

I know what happened after that. I don't even have to ask but I do anyway. "So they went to jail, started pointing fingers and hit Bailey?"

Fabian nods. "And that's where it stops. He's in on a conspiracy charge. In the long run, the middle man has enough plausible deniability that his charges stayed small. All that was left was a respected attorney and a decorated cop. Bailey's from a long line of goodfellas. Even if he thought anyone would believe him, he wouldn't snitch."

He bows his head in a brief moment of thought before he continues. "Windy, I know it sounds like shit coming from me, but I'm sorry. I never would have started if I knew how it would end."

I don't believe him. That is to say that he seems sincere enough, but his nerve is through the roof. "You're sorry?" I have to laugh. "My mom is dead. You're free. *And* you're a hell of a lot richer, I'm sure. And to top it all off, all this time you've been waving your disapproving finger at me, and then you sit back and watch me clean up your loose ends. You're the worst kind of lying bastard."

He's quiet for a few seconds and I hear him stand up. If I know Fabian, he's straightening his tie and checking his hair. That's his usual routine.

"I miss her eyes," he reflects as he moves around to where I sit on the floor, my back still to the desk. "She had the most beautiful eyes. You have them too, you know."

I want more than anything to kill him right now. But I can't. I can't kill him. Everyone I've ever killed… I was just cleaning up his mess. If I kill him, I'll just be cleaning up somebody else's mess. Somebody else's loose ends. Somebody else… Oh shit.

"Fabian," I say, feeling his gaze turn toward me even though I don't meet it. "Who's the cop?"

My question is answered with three

sounds: a click, the sound of the door opening; a bang, the sound of a gun firing; and a thump, the sound of Fabian's lifeless body collapsing beside me with a bullet hole above his left eye.

Fuck.

I swore to myself I would never be caught unaware. I would always have a plan for every possible situation. I would always be ready.

I'm not ready for this.

Fabian's dead. If I don't think quickly, I will be too. Think fast. I need to think fast. I need to stop thinking about thinking fast and just think fast.

He only saw Fabian.

I drop to my side and roll onto my stomach, peering across the cheap carpet under the desk to see a pair of Hush Puppies pacing around the other side. I feel like a cat ready to pounce with my eyes leveled across the ground and my ass hanging into the empty air behind me. But as much as I want to spring over the desk and claw at his face, I know that I'll be dead as soon as the first stray hair is visible over the desktop.

I hold my crouch as I creep around, keeping the desk directly between me and Mr. Hush Puppies as I watch his slow, steady stride.

He stops when he reaches Fabian's body.

What's he doing? Looking down, surveying his handiwork? Doesn't matter. His back is turned to me. I've been in this office a thousand times, so I'm able to back my way toward the door without looking. The only concern I have at the moment is that he isn't looking either. He crouches down over the body. I presume he's checking a pulse. Again, it doesn't matter. I quicken my pace, trying to keep silent as I move in reverse.

Before I know it, my knees are on tile as I reach the hallway. I try to move even more smoothly, knowing that one knee falling too hard will attract his attention. One toe sliding across tile will give me away. I know there's an office to the left and I back my way into it at the very same moment that Mr. Hush Puppies stands up.

Part of me wants him to turn around so that I can see his face. But I know that will reveal me to him too.

There are five other doors that I need to work my way through before I can get to the lobby. Do I have time before he starts coming down the hallway? Can I steal a peak at his face without him knowing that I'm here? Should I hide behind a desk and wait for him to go?

No waiting. I don't know when or even if he's going to leave. I can't hide out and wait for him to find me and kill me. Down the hall is my only option. And there's no sense in getting away if I don't know who I'm getting away from. That leaves me hopeless all over again.

So I peer through the crack between the door and the frame, only to be met with nothing. No side of the face, no back of the head, no Hush Puppies, nothing. What that tells me is that it's time to move.

I can't shuffle across. Too much noise. I can't get to my feet. Again, too much noise. I guess it comes back down to crawling.

I back out from behind the door and make my way across the hall to the next office down the line. I've made it out of two rooms in a total of seven, much more quickly than I ever would have thought I could. Now I'm in danger of getting cocky. I rotate myself around to peer through the crack of another doorframe. This time I get the back of a head as I assume he's sifting through the mess of papers occupying the top of Fabian's desk.

If I'm quick enough, I can make it across the hallway again before he turns his head. So quickly is how I move as I back away from the doorframe, eager to make my move and find myself moving the back of my skull directly into the doorknob. I bite my tongue but I already know that the small impact made enough of a noise to attract attention. All I can do now is get out from behind the door so that when he turns his head he won't see my eyes.

This office is just like the other six, so I move as swiftly and quietly as possible to the other side of the desk.

Historically, panic has always been a great motivator. It gets the blood flowing, the adrenaline pumping, it forces a person to make things happen. The problem is that what it motivates is very rarely well planned. It is rash, abrupt, and in cases of life and death, tends to push a person closer to death then it does to life. In my case, I've just managed to trap myself behind a desk mere minutes after escaping the same situation.

This time I'm in for the long haul, so I actually pull the chair out and crawl underneath the desk. The only way out of this is if he's distracted and I can find some kind of magical opportunity or if he just doesn't notice me and decides that it was all part of his imagination. I'm not banking on either one of those things happening, which leads to option number three: he finds me and kills me.

The hallway is quiet enough to hear a pin drop, but the only sounds I hear are the footfalls of Mr. Hush Puppies. Very slow, very soft, very careful. Then his footsteps halt and it sounds like he's rifling through his pockets. In a moment I hear a voice that I suspected I would hear, though I've been hoping it wouldn't be true.

"I've got an incident at the offices of Fabian Winston," comes the voice of Detective Jerry Leonard. "We're gonna need the coroner down here. I've got two bodies."

Two bodies? My first thought is that poor Julia never made it out. Collateral damage is too sloppy, though. They're trying to clean up a mess, not make a new one. No, the second body is mine. And I'm trapped underneath a desk, waiting for the inevitable.

I hear Hush Puppies slowly coming out of Fabian's office. "Windy?"

You can't be serious. Does he expect me to answer?

"Honey, the police are still ten minutes out," he starts. I hear his voice quiet as he enters the other office across the hall. "That gives me more than enough time to find you."

He's trying to bait me. To reveal my position. I'm breathing too hard, too fast. I have to slow down or he'll hear me for sure.

"Your mother was a good woman," he starts again. "I'm sure Fabian told you… It wasn't meant to be her. We had no idea."

Footsteps. He's searching for my hiding spot. He knows I won't give myself up. Still he baits me.

"The damn harvesters weren't picky," his voice is getting closer. "They didn't care who they picked up as long as they matched the right blood type." He's leaving the other office. Next stop: here.

"I thought your dad would be a little bit stronger, though."

I want to kill him. I want to leave my hiding spot and wrap my fingers around his neck. But then I'm out in the open and he wins. He's coming into the office now. I've slowed my breathing down but if my heart beats any faster it's going to pound a hole through the desk.

"He just kinda curled up into a ball and hid from the world, didn't he?"

I can hear his footsteps coming closer. His Hush Puppies are peaking under the desk into my little cubby hole. Another inch and he would have kicked me. I'm about thirty seconds from being discovered. If I don't do something very quickly, I'm going to die. Despite everything that I've found out about myself and my life today, I really don't want that to happen.

"I guess that's something you and he have in common," he baits me one last time. It works this time.

The action comes without thinking. I press my hands against the bottom of the desk and brace my shoulders in the same way. All at once I stand up and push the desk forward, forcing it directly into the detective's upper torso and face. It has the desired effect.

When the blur of motion has passed, all that I see when I look down are a pair of legs sticking out from underneath the overturned desk reminiscent of the Wizard of Oz. You know, if the witch wore khakis and penny loafers.

He should be stunned long enough for me to get away, and I need to move as quickly as possible because the munchkins should be arriving any minute now.

I take two strides toward him, step up onto the edge of the desk, and as I hear him groan under the collective weight of the desk and my body pushing down on his torso, I jump to the floor on the other side. As I pass over, I glance down at the face that I've put so much trust in for so long now. I officially have no one left.

When I hit the floor, I find Riley's gun laying directly between my foot and Jerry's hand. I left it on the floor in Fabian's office. That was sloppy of me. Jerry was going to kill me with it. Turnabout is fair play.

I pick up the revolver and point it at Jerry's face. He stares up at me, his gaze meeting mine. Without breaking eye contact, he forces the words out the best he can with a desk on top of him. "Do it," he says. "I would."

"I know you would," I reply. "You tried."

I want to. More than anything I want to. I kneel down and press the barrel to his forehead. I pull back the hammer. My whole body shakes as I think about pulling the trigger and the immense satisfaction it would give to my rage. I press the barrel down hard as tears begin to bleed through the anger.

He just stares at me.

I stand up and slowly replace the hammer on the revolver. As I wipe away the tears, I glare so intently at his face what I feel as though I'll burn holes through his cheeks.

"I hate you," I tell him, "more than words

could ever express. But I'm not you."

With that I turn and run down the hall. Julia's not in the lobby. I didn't think she would be, but my heartbeat slows down just a bit when I'm able to verify it. I bypass the elevator and head straight to the stairwell. As the door closes behind me I can hear the *bing* signaling the opening of the elevator doors. The police have arrived.

I make it down the stairs and out of the building without instance. I admire their efficiency. They've just arrived and already all of the police are on Fabian's floor which leaves an empty lobby and a clear path.

I'm through the door and looking for the car right away. I find it quickly and make my way there without a single witness. Now I'm waiting.

And waiting.

And waiting.

After a little over an hour, Detective Leonard emerges from the building with a younger officer trailing behind. I hear bits of the conversation.

"You didn't think to check for a pulse before calling in the second body?" It's the younger officer speaking.

Jerry looks frustrated. I guess he should have made sure I was dead before he started telling others about it. "I guess it was there, just too weak to feel."

"Too weak? We found you under a desk!" The younger seems kind of flustered himself. "Look, I'm just saying your story's got holes. I don't know why that is. I really don't give a fuck. But get your shit straight and get it straight quick. I.A. is gonna have questions. If you're solid then you're gonna be okay. But you're not solid right now. You're not even jello. You're all over the place."

They get to Jerry's car and Jerry opens the door, looking over it at the younger detective. He takes a deep breath before answering. "Look, Paul, you're right. I'm just shaken up, I guess. My head's all crazy trying to get blood flow to the lower half of my body again."

"Alright," Paul says, "get some lunch, get your head straight, and for god's sake calm the fuck down. Find me at the precinct in an hour and we'll redo your statement."

Jerry smiles. I can't see it but I can hear it in his voice. "You're too good to me, Paul. Alright, I'll see you in an hour."

He sits down in the driver seat and closes

the door of his company car. You know the unmarked police cars, the plain looking sedans with ten antennae, flood lights and the windows tinted so dark that there's no way in hell he could have seen me waiting for him in the back seat? Yeah it's one of those.

I touch the revolver to the back of his neck. He jumps.

"Hey Jerry," I say. "What's for lunch?"

His eyes meet mine in the rearview. "You won't shoot," he says. "If you wanted to kill me then you would've done it in the hallway."

"I've had some time to think," I explain. "I think I've found my motivation."

I felt like an orphan. My mother had been dead two weeks and though I still had my father, he was dead to the world. In the first few days after losing mom he seemed okay. The shock had not set in yet. On the third day, we held the memorial service. When we got home he went into the master bath and didn't come out. For the first day I left him alone. He needed time. I got that. When the morning came and he still hadn't emerged, I begged and pleaded and banged on the door for him to come out, even if it was just to eat. And he eventually did. I brought him food and he devoured it without a word, without anything more than a blank stare. When he had finished eating he managed to push out a word of gratitude before disappearing into the bathroom again. The next ten days went the same way. I had occasional visits from my mother's friends or Fabian or Detective Leonard checking up on me, but dad only came out to eat, and generally only once a day. Fifteen days after my mother's death, my dad didn't respond. I pounded, I yelled, I cried, I begged. I turned the doorknob. It wasn't locked. I pushed the door open. The bathtub was full and my dad lay face down inside it. I really was an orphan.

Twelve

The elevator door slides open onto the floor of Riley's penthouse. Jerry never stopped talking for the entire drive here. He's impressed at how much I accomplished; thanks for cleaning up his loose ends; thanks for distracting Fabian and giving him a clean shot; it's a good thing he was always the lead investigator so he could clean up *my* loose ends; and so on and so forth.

In fact, he doesn't shut up until we get to Riley's office. There sits Riley, exactly as I left him, behind the desk and complete with bullet hole placed just right so that it looks like the top of his nose sports a third nostril.

Jerry stops in his tracks. "Windy," he begins to speak, "I..."

"You just did the same thing to Fabian and were about to do it to me," I interrupt. "Not to mention that Fabian tried to set Riley up to shoot me himself. I suppose you knew about that, though."

Jerry considers for a moment before he says, "It was actually my idea. I knew he wouldn't be able to kill you. You took it on yourself to take out the buyers, everyone that could finger Winston. Bailey was the last one. I thought giving him the gun would give you that last little push you needed to make sure you finished. With Bailey gone, there was nobody left that could get a sudden attack of conscience and identify Winston. And the only one who could identify me was him. So I fixed it.

"You weren't supposed to be there. You were supposed to be done after Bailey. Killing you was never part of the plan. I would cover up key pieces of evidence one last time and we would both walk away from this mess. We still can."

I leave him where he stands and walk toward the desk where Riley sits. "Don't bullshit me, Jerry. That gets you out of this situation, but the next chance you get you'll kill me."

The detective doesn't speak for a few seconds. When he finally does, he takes a step toward me and asks, "So how did you find out about Winston? Bailey couldn't hold his tongue?"

"I actually had to beat it out of him," I

answer. "He kept his mouth shut well enough. Fabian ruined the surprise." I set the revolver down on the desk, just where Riley had set it when he and I had talked earlier. I pick up his phone and run my fingers over the screen before holding it up to show Jerry. "The last phone call was from Fabian Winston. I answered it."

I circle around the desk, running my fingers across the touchscreen one more time before coming around behind Riley and dropping the phone into his shirt pocket. Well, it mostly fits into his pocket. It's a big phone so the end protrudes just over the pocket's rim.

Jerry chuckles. "I knew that guy was a liability. I should have killed him sooner but I needed to make sure Bailey was dead first. You would have known something was wrong if something happened to Winston."

I walk toward him, glaring. "Because I don't know that something's wrong as it is?"

He doesn't answer my question, only asks, "So what happens now?"

"Now," I reply, "is when you tell all of the other people with shiny badges exactly what you've done."

I'm only a foot away from him now. He's trying to stare me down. It's not working.

"Oh yeah, Jerry," I continue, "You're going to tell them about all the deaths you're responsible for."

Jerry lets out a short laugh. "All of the deaths that *I'm* responsible for?"

I nod. We stare at each other for a few moments and then before I even realize that he's moving, his hand is against the side of my head. Things blur and I find myself leaning against a wall and spitting blood. My left ear is ringing where he hit me. The floor is moving. Why is the floor moving?

He's talking but I don't hear it like I should be hearing it.

"...leave the gun right where you put it. It won't be necessary."

I can't tell where his voice is coming from but I know he has to be coming toward me. When I look down at the moving floor, a foot appears in my line of sight. He's on my left. I have to do something.

In attempting what is supposed to be a punch, I fling my entire body to where I think he is. I miss. My body falls limp on the floor. I feel a sharp pain in the top of my head as my hair is wrapped around Jerry's hand and pulled.

He's dragging me across the room. I'm

flailing my legs around not to get away but to escape the friction burns I'm getting on my calves. I'm finally starting to get focus. My ears are clearing. He's still talking.

"You're right, Windy," he says. "I have to tell everyone about all of the blood on my hands."

We reach the desk and he yanks me to my knees. I can see over the top of the desk, but it's still moving. I can see Riley sitting on the other side. I can see the revolver right in front of me. If my reflexes were normal then I could reach up and grab it. As it is, I can barely move my arms at all.

"Let's start with Madame Serenade," he says. "That was pretty brutal. How did I do that one? Was it like this?"

His grip tightens on my hair and he pushes my face into the desk. And again. And again. I lose count. Even if I could distinguish between the hits, I don't think I'd be able to remember the numbers or the order to count them in.

Eventually the hits stop. I can't tell if my head is resting on my chin or on its side. I open my eyes to try to get my bearings but Riley's lifeless body is swinging in front of me like a pendulum.

I see motion behind Riley. The detective is circling. Waiting until I regain some focus before he makes the next move. I hope the focus never comes. I hope the room keeps spinning... spinning... round and round...

My head slides off of the desk and I vomit on the way to the floor. One more head impact. There's moisture between my head and the floor. I can't tell if it's blood or vomit. I don't care.

I'm looking at Riley's feet now. If I focus on the feet, it feels like the rest of the room isn't spinning so wildly. Focus on the feet. Focus on the feet. He's holding my hair again. He's pulling me to my knees. He's talking again.

"What about Todd?" he asks. "That one was pretty straightforward. Concealed sharp object... stab wound..."

As he says the last two words I feel a sharp pain in my shoulder. When he pulls it out I can see the spinning image of a letter opener. He plunges it in again, this time on the side. I manage to follow the weapon as it pulls out again. And again it comes toward my chest. This time I don't even know where it hits. I feel the pain but I can't discern one wound from the next.

I can't move. I'm still on my knees but

facing away from the desk now. It feels like even falling down would take too much effort. I don't know where he is. All I can do is wait for him to come back into my line of sight. All I can do is wait for the next dose of karma. Here it comes.

He appears in front of me again, this time holding the revolver. "And now let's see if I can recall how exactly it was that I killed Mr. Bailey. Ah yes. The old classic gunshot wound to the head."

Jerry raises the barrel of the gun and points it at my face. He steps closer and closer until all of the pain in my body is replaced with only the feeling of cold metal between my eyes. I feel it all through my body. My eyes and ears clear instantly as I watch and listen to the revolver's hammer being pulled back.

He stares into my eyes and his mouth opens to speak but no words come out for what seems like forever. When they finally do, all I can hear is, "You never should have answered that phone."

And then I hear the shot, as if time slows down and wants to give me one final bit of agony before the bullet ends it. But the bullet never comes. The pain never comes. I expect the world to turn black, but instead I see the revolver fall away from my face and watch as a red circle forms on Jerry's shoulder and slowly grows.

The revolver drops to the floor and so does the detective. His image is replaced by that of Paul, the younger detective that Jerry had been talking to outside of Fabian's office. My vision is tilting again, but I see the younger man putting handcuffs on the older one.

He turns his head to look at me and says something that I can't make out. Through the pain, through the disorientation, I become aware that falling down doesn't feel like quite so much effort anymore.

I sat in the police station one week after my father's death in the office of Detective Leonard. He had taken a special interest in me. It seemed as though he felt obligated to make sure that I was okay. So much had happened to me in so short a time and he was there for all of it. It seemed like I spent a lot of time in that office. I didn't really know where else to go. On this particular day, he had asked me in. He said that he had news to share. He brought me a cup of coffee, sat down at his desk, and started talking. "Windy, I know it's not much for consolation, but I wanted you to know that we now have in custody all of the men involved in your abduction." "All of them?" I asked. "How many were there?" "All together, about twenty two. They were a whole organization all the way from the surgeons to the kidnappers, the delivery guys, the salesmen... For what they did, they accomplished a whole lot with not a lot of people." "You'll forgive me if I don't find it as impressive as you." He caught himself, "I know. I'm sorry. The important thing is that we get them all. And if you feel up to testifying, it should be a really quick and easy trial." "Of course," I say, "I'll do whatever I can to help." I pause for a moment before asking, "So is it done then? Nobody's going to have to go through what I did?" The detective sighed. "Well, we put a very productive ring out of commission. That's huge. But when all is said and done, as long as there are people willing to purchase organs, there are going to be people willing to sell them." He picked a small piece of paper up off of the desk, held it up and said, "These are the three people who purchased the pieces of your mom. Unfortunately, there's not much we can do to prosecute the buyers. But these are the people who create the demand. These are the people that the criminals really work for. As long as people like this are willing to spend big money, this won't ever stop happening." He put the list back down on the desk with a heavy sigh. And the very first time he turned around, I put that same list into my pocket.

Epilogue

I wake up in the hospital. I don't know which hospital. I don't know what day or time it is. The one thing that immediately strikes me is that I'm alone. Though I don't know what else I expected.

I find the button to call the nurse and I press it. A voice outside the doors tells me that she'll be right in. When that promise is made good, it's not just the nurse that enters but also a young detective named Paul.

The doctor tells me that I had severe head trauma and significant blood loss from several wounds. I've been unconscious for the better part of a week. As much as I'd like for the whole ordeal to have been a dream, I peek under my gown and see the mass of bandages that tell me I'm going to have scars resembling the size and shape of a letter opener's blade.

When the doctor finishes telling me that

I'm going to live, Paul takes his turn to tell me just how lucky I am. Jerry is apparently blaming all of the murders on me. Go figure. But there was apparently a video streaming from Riley's phone straight to the police department, showing Detective Leonard confessing to the murders while torturing me. According to Paul, the judge handling Jerry's arraignment referred to it as 'damning evidence.'

I'll be expected to testify, though the aforementioned 'damning evidence' really makes it wholly unnecessary. In two days I'll be allowed to go home. In truth, I don't know what that means anymore. I've spent my entire adult life so far preparing for and hunting down people that I had no reason to hunt down. No real reason, at least.

Maybe I'll do all the things that I wanted to do before any of this happened.

Maybe I'll cure cancer.

Maybe I'll really meet a guy and go on a real date.

Maybe I'll find the paparazzi waiting outside the front doors of the hospital and I'll take them out to Starbucks.

One way or another, I suppose it's time for me to be a real person now. Whatever that might mean.

Almost five years after my parents' death, I sat in an apartment downtown waiting. For almost five years I'd paid attention to only three people. For almost five years I made plans and considered everything that might go wrong, everything that might come up. And for every plan, I had a backup. For almost five years I practiced becoming exactly the kind of person that my mom wanted me to be. I went to every party I was invited to, which inevitably got me invited to more parties. I bought the right people drinks, danced with the right people and held the right people's hair as they puked into the right people's toilets. I finally understood the power that my mom had tried so hard to teach me through all of her social networking skills. It's not something I had ever wanted, but it was something I learned and something I took advantage of. I was the celebrity that was famous for the sake of being famous. Famous based on who I knew, which was pretty close to everyone in the world. I could get through almost any door I wanted and I could get a date with any guy I wanted. And so when Fabian tried to set me up on a blind date, the gentleman caller jumped at the chance to spend an evening with Windswept Rohm. He was a perfect gentleman for the entire night. I almost wished that our date had been made under different circumstances. But it wasn't. And so after an enjoyable evening of dinner and dancing and leading my new friend back to an apartment that I specifically rented for this very evening (and that I most certainly did not use my real name for), we kissed good night and, knowing that I let off all the right signs, I waited by the door for Todd to come back. And I knew for sure that he would. I gave off all the right signs. I told him what a good time I had. And now I waited for the knock. I waited for him to come back. I knew he was coming back. I had planned it down to the second. And the seconds were running out. I counted them down.

Four...

Three...

Two...

One...

Knock knock knock.

Patrick Quin Kermott's published works to date include the stories *George Morgan Associates* and *Chris*. The novella *Windswept Rohm,* originally released under the title *Sex and Violence,* is his first full length work.

Patrick spent his childhood and the early parts of adulthood in Southern California before fleeing to the White Mountains of Arizona where he currently lives with his wife, Lindsay, and three sons, Isaiah, Ezekiel and Lazarus.